OF WOLVES & WITCHES

ARCANE ARTS ACADEMY: BOOK 1

ELENA LAWSON

1

———

That thieving bastard.

Did he really think I hadn't seen him stuff the necklace into his sleeve? My teeth clenched and a furious heat sizzled down my spine, pooling in my stomach like acid. And who the hell wore a long-sleeve shirt in this weather, anyway? Even in a tank top with a headband holding back my long hair—my forehead was still varnished in a tacky layer of sweat.

The creep peeked up at me under his black and blue hair, smirking, before going back to leisurely 'browsing' through the wares at our booth. Picking up another necklace, before placing it back down to fiddle with the potions, reading their attached tags.

They told me it would be easy when they left this morning. Putting me in charge of our tiny stall right at the heart of the French Market. *It shouldn't be too busy,* they said, *you'll be fine.*

But they were wrong. The city square had come alive in the few hours it'd been since dawn. The sun came out to play, and with it came the morning shoppers and the fanny-pack-toting tourists. I groaned.

Any excuse to go to New Orleans had my guardians here in an instant, speeding the old caravan down I-65 while singing about country roads and open highways. Lots of witches made New Orleans their home. It was easier to blend in when there were palminsters, psychics, and occult shops all over the place. Made it harder to decipher fakes from the real thing.

It was accepted here—or at least *tolerated.*

So, I understood why they liked it so much. Less hiding. And even the earth under the soles of my flip-flops seemed to buzz with power like nowhere else, eagerly waiting to answer a witch's call.

Where are they? I looked over the heads of the throng of people, the heady scent of roasting meat and the tang of fresh oranges wafting over from the food vendors.

The smooth rhythm of sax and guitar rose from where two buskers played for nickels and dimes in the square. I couldn't see them anywhere. *Damn.* I set my jaw. Guess I'd have to deal with the douche myself…

Clenching my hand into a fist, I drew in a deep breath, squashing my body's instinctual reflex to draw magic.

"Uh—hello? Anybody home?" the nasally voice broke my concentration and I cleared my throat, turning to find two chicks in their early twenties. Both icey-blond with honey-colored eyes—showing off a generous amount of their perfectly bronzed skin.

"Did you hear what I said?" the one on the right whined.

I eyed the guy still sifting through our booth— running his immoral fingers over the rings Leo had crafted the week before, lifting one to inspect the topaz gemstone.

Don't even think about it…

He put the ring back down. But the weight in his sleeve seemed larger than it was a moment before. I took a steadying breath.

I'd deal with him in a minute.

"No, I'm sorry, what did you say?" I answered blonde number one in a rush, keeping a wary eye on the thief.

She huffed, holding up a potion bottle filled with a shimmery red liquid, matching her perfectly mani-cured crimson nails. "Does this stuff work?" she asked, her brows narrowing as she shook the lust potion in front of my face. "And, like, did *you* brew it? Or was it brewed by—you know, like, an *actual* witch?"

An *actual* witch? Was this bimbo serious?

There were true Alchemists and then there were those who attempted to replicate our natural abilities with crude science. They made some admirable attempts, but never quite accomplished the things they set out to do.

Metal into gold? Even I could do that with a simple sigil and I'm only seventeen and technically not allowed to practice underage magic, at least not without proper adult supervision.

But alas, it was frowned upon to use our abilities for direct monetary gain in mortal society.

Pretty much all the fun stuff is forbidden.

Philosopher's stone? Well, once our people had the knowledge and the formula to do it— passed down through generations, but it was lost somewhere along the way from our homeland of Emeris to our new home in the mortal lands. But I really don't think people should live forever anyway, and we live longer than most already.

I smiled sweetly at the pair of them. "Of course I didn't brew it," I answered her, clasping my hands together at my front. "It was made by the Wicked

Witch of the West at the stroke of midnight under the light of a full moon."

Blonde number one sneered at me, curling a pink lip over blinding white teeth while blond number two's eyes widened, backing away from her friend. "You think you're *so* edgy in that baggy tank top with your stubby nails and your pale skin and that *obviously* dyed red hair? Well, you're not… And you just lost a paying customer," Blonde number one sniveled, tossing the potion back onto the table. "Come on Fiona, lets go get a smoothie."

I wanted to shout after her. Tell her my bright red hair wasn't dyed, and that I could see her ass hanging out of her shorts as she walked away. But it wouldn't be worth my time. *Ignorant humans.* Must be nice to not have to live in hiding. Afraid to be yourself. Avoiding discovery at every turn.

They were probably born and raised here.

I didn't even know where I was born. And I was raised in the back of Leo and Lara's caravan after a human woman begged them to take me when I was barely six months old. All I knew was what she told them. That my father was a witch and he was dead. That she was my human mother and didn't know the first thing about raising a witch. She never said how she knew Leo and Lara were witches.

The woman left me with them, and she never came back.

It was no wonder I'd lost all respect for humanity. Girls like that just solidified my views. Selfish, cowardly creatures.

And they thought *we* were the monsters. What a joke.

Scowling, I turned back to the booth—my spine going rigid. Where did he go? Magic buzzed in my veins. An innate defense mechanism I shoved deep down—attempting to bury it.

I scanned the crowded market space, spotting a black haired head with a streak of blue running through it.

Got you now, sucker.

I darted after him, throwing a half-assed warding spell up in my wake to try to keep shoppers away from the booth. I weaved through the bodies in my way, almost losing sight of him as he neared the food vendors.

The guy looked back, catching sight of me chasing him. Our eyes locked. And then he ran.

"Hey!" I shouted after him, spurring myself to go faster. "Hey! Thief! Stop that guy!"

A hundred sets of eyes turned to the sound of my shouting voice, but none moved to help me. *Useless.*

Sweat dropped down my back, and my flip-flops slapped the pavement. Nearing the exit to the market, he sped up. *No!* If he got outside, I'd lose him for sure.

And who knew how much more stuff he stole while I wasn't paying attention. *Stupid.*

I moved to cut him off through the fruit market and ran smack into a pyramid of apples, scattering them to the floor.

"Sorry!" I called back to the shopkeeper who was shouting obscenities after me.

Crap, crap, crap!

Why did I always have to mess shit up?

My chest squeezing, I darted between two booths and missed him by a hair. He blew past me into the main square, shoving people out of his way without a care.

"Stop!" I screamed at him, beyond furious. The familiar crackle of energy under my skin wouldn't be soothed, no matter how much I tried to swallow it down.

He was too fast. I'd never catch him. And then I'd have to deal with their disappointment *again.* I'd have to explain how I messed up. They wouldn't be surprised. They'd say they *knew* I wasn't ready to have the responsibility of running the booth.

My body opened to the energy running through the earth like blood through veins. Hauling it in like the first breath after coming up from the water.

"*Stop!*" I shouted again, and the ground shook

beneath my feet. A great groan had me skidding to a stop. My hands shook.

Crack! The pavement split. A fissure slicing through it from where I stood, skittering out over the square. Chasing the thief down faster than I ever could.

Someone screamed.

The sky darkened, and my blood boiled.

The fissure reached him, and he grunted as the ground heaved under his feet, sending him sprawling into the street. The jewelry jolted from his sleeve to land unceremoniously on the road beside him.

Cars screeched to a standstill. Their horns blaring. People everywhere were shouting. Running. *Earthquake,* they said, but they were wrong.

The magic I'd used still coursed through me, slowly waning. Leaching out of my bones to return to the earth, leaving me shivering against a sudden chill.

The ground still pulsed beneath my feet. My fists clenched.

What have I done?

Across the street stood two men. They weren't running away. Or trying to film the scene. They weren't even looking at the giant gash in the pavement.

They were staring at me.

2

The thief stumbled to his feet before scurrying away like a rat, leaving the jewelry behind.

But he didn't matter anymore. And neither did the few hundred dollars' worth of silver and gems.

The taller of the two men turned his wrist to face me. The golden tattoo shimmered in the warm morning light. A triangle with two crossed arrows. My breath hitched, and I worked to quell the tremble in my knees.

Arcane Authorities.

Bad luck seemed to be as irrevocably attached to me as my own shadow, but this really took the cake. Was there any way they hadn't seen what I did?

The shorter one with the tight jaw and thick brows met my wide-eyed stare. He tilted his head toward a shaded alley before the two of them stepped out of the light and into the shadows, waiting for me to follow them.

Nope. They definitely saw.

I could run, but chances were I wouldn't get far before they caught me. And then what? Running would only get me into more trouble.

No, running wasn't an option. I sighed—stuffing my hands into the pockets of my shorts. Leo and Lara were right. It was only a matter of time before my magic got me into trouble, but I'd make sure they didn't go down with me.

The traffic started to move again once I'd crossed the street. The people had gone back to their shopping and gossiping, avoiding the split in the pavement.

They'd fix it. Fill it in. It would be like it never happened for them.

I had a feeling I wouldn't be so lucky. I steeled myself before stepping into the alley, a million thoughts tripping and swirling through my mind.

I'm too young to be sent to Kalzir Prison… and besides, that place was reserved for murderers and dark witches, not for people who accidently cleaved the earth in two… right?

It was true being underage would save *me* from Kalzir, but it would be Leo and Lara who were punished for my unsupervised use of magic.

"We haven't got all day," a deep accented voice rang out from the alley, and I hurriedly stepped inside, feeling the kiss of energy against my skin as a ward snapped into place behind me. Sealing us off from the curious eyes of the outside world.

I jumped at the sensation, turning in time to see the taller of the two flicking his finger as he finished drawing a binding sigil in midair, the swirling, looping pattern glowing a bright orange. He shoved his palm against it and the sigil expanded and then vanished, settling over me like a wave of concrete.

My hands flew behind my back, my fingers clasping of their own accord. The spell was even stronger than the time I accidentally crazy-glued my hands together. I couldn't move them at all. There was no sense in struggling and yet I couldn't help trying.

"Wait, please!" I said, my voice wavering. "I can explain—"

"And you will," said the one with the thick brows. "But it isn't us you'll need to do your explaining to."

Neither moved to take hold of me, but instead maintained their distance at about ten paces away at the dead-end of brick wall. The taller one swallowed, his gaze darting from me back to his partner. He seemed… afraid? Of what?

Surely, they weren't afraid of *me?*

I mean, my magic hadn't ever caused a minor earthquake before. I mostly did simple spells, but even I had to admit they never turned out how I intended. Like the time I tried to use magic to extinguish a candle and put out every fire at the campground instead…. Or when I made potions that didn't work *exactly* like they were expected to.

"Where are your parents?" The shorter one asked.

I looked away, my heart thumping wildly in my chest. An image of my guardians flashed in my mind.

Lie, my subconscious screamed.

"I don't have any parents," I told them, weaving honesty into the lie. "They're dead."

Thick Brows scowled. "So, you're all alone, then?"

I bit the inside of my cheek and nodded. My eyes burned.

They'd be so worried when they saw I was gone. Would I be able to return to them? I didn't know what happened to underage witches with no parents or guardians. But I could not, under any circumstances, bring the authorities back to our booth.

Selling potions to humans was illegal, and though I had no problem with it—especially since they were weakened versions of the real thing—the Arcane Council would see it a *little* differently. If the

Arcane Authorities saw their booth, it would earn my guardians a one-way ticket to Kalzir…

My hands came apart and I looked up to find Tall Guy frowning, a gleam of pity in his eyes. "You won't give us any trouble, will you?" he asked.

I shook my head. "I swear I didn't mean to—"

"Didn't mean to?" Thick Brows interrupted. "That was strong magic. Not just anyone could've pulled that off."

"What's your name?" the other one asked, inching closer, looking more at ease than he did before.

My skin bristled. "Harper… just Harper."

"Well, 'just Harper,' I'm afraid your fate is now in the hands of the Arcane Council."

My blood chilled and the spark of magic reignited in my blood.

"Try to stay calm," the taller one added. "Everything will be fine."

Why did I get the feeling he was lying to my face?

I didn't dare speak. Afraid I'd burst into tears or wind up begging for freedom I knew they wouldn't give me. Tall Guy was right—I had to stay calm. Bad things happened when I wasn't calm. I didn't want to add any more to the list of crimes I'd already committed.

And to think it wasn't even noon.

Must be some sort of record.

Thick Brows set to work drawing out a sigil on the brick wall behind them. I was still crap at them, but I recognized the symbol for travel, and the one for creating a doorway interwoven with others I didn't recognize. He was opening a portal.

"Come," he said, and the brick disintegrated before my eyes to reveal a long hallway with a parquet floor and golden sconces that cast a rich umber light on the mahogany wood paneling. It looked like the inside of a castle.

My stomach dropped.

A loud *meow* set my hair standing on edge, and I flinched. Relief flood through me at the sight of the orange tabby jumping down from the rooftop above onto a trash bin against the wall.

"Your familiar?" Thick Brows asked.

I shook my head as Gato, Leo's familiar, pounced down to rub himself against my legs. "No, he isn't mine."

"Then hurry up, would you? I can't hold the doorway open all day."

I bent down to scratch the tuft of fur under his jaw. If Gato was here that meant Leo and Lara weren't far. I had to go before they found me… and the Arcane Authorities who had me under arrest. With a lump in my throat, I whispered to him. "Tell them not to come looking for me."

The cat stopped, sitting back to listen. "They'll be punished if they do, and I—I'd never forgive myself."

Gato growled, turning to hiss at the men still waiting at the wall.

I hushed him, dropping my voice lower to make sure they couldn't hear. "I'll be alright. And I'll be back as soon as I can. Now go."

The cat jumped back up onto the trash can and then up to the roof, turning back to look at me only for a moment before he vanished from sight. I hoped they'd understand.

"Let's go—"

Before he could finish, I crossed my arms, bent my head, and stomped down the alley and through the portal. My jaw clenched tight to stop the stinging in the back of my throat.

THE ARCANE AUTHORITY guys had just finished explaining to the Council delegate—a man with graying brown hair, kind eyes, and a thick southern accent—what I'd done.

"Given that she's underage with no guardians, we thought it a matter best handled by the council directly."

The older man huffed from the other side of the ornate wooden desk separating us. "Yes, yes," he said, waving them off, never once taking his milky gaze from me. "Thank you, that'll be all."

Thick Brows stiffened. Likely, they weren't used to being so easily dismissed. But they left without another word, closing the large double doors to the office behind them with a solemn click.

"Now then," the delegate of the Arcane Council smiled, showing two rows of yellowed teeth between his thin lips. "Are you often able to produce magic in such… magnitude?"

I tucked my hands between my knees to stop them from vibrating as I spoke. Did my best to meet his gaze with a steady one of my own. "No. I don't know what happened."

"You needn't lie to me, girl," he said, cocking his head to one side as he considered me. Something in his expression, or maybe in the way he'd said it made me believe him. Maybe if I told him the truth, he'd understand it wasn't my fault I couldn't control it.

"Sometimes," I amended, not able to decide one way or the other if I should trust the old man. There were twelve delegates that made up the Arcane Council, and a Magistrate that had the final say on the important things. My mind was still reeling with the fact that I now sat in the office of one of the most powerful men in the witching community.

He could have me imprisoned. Killed. The most likely thing to happen would be to be stripped of all my powers, which, honestly, wouldn't be all that bad.

"Thought so," he mused, making a clucking sound with his tongue as he rolled the information around in his mind.

Sweat beaded at my hairline despite the cool air in the dusky office. It was so silent you could hear a pin drop. As though all the sound in the universe had been vacuumed up, blocked out by the insulation of hundreds upon hundreds of tomes lining thick wooden shelves all around the space.

I shook off the miasmal feeling. I wished he'd just get on with it. There was no sense in dragging this out. I was sure he'd already decided on what my punishment would be. But you didn't rush an Arcane Council member.

"Who were your parents?" he asked after a time, and I flinched at the question, sucking in a quick, sharp breath.

"I'm not sure. They died when I was very small," I said, giving a small shrug. "I never knew their names."

It wasn't total bullshit. I didn't know my mother's name, but I knew my father's. Alistair was his name. I only knew it because it was inscribed on the inside of the ring my mother left with me. A gawdy golden thing with a great bird on it. An orange colored stone where its eye should've been. His last name began with an H, but the engraving was worn down from too many years of wear. I glanced down at it, twisting it round my thumb—the only finger it fit.

The delegate seemed intrigued by the ring but snapped out of his glazed over stare when I shoved my hands back between my knees. He cleared his throat. "A pity," he began, pursing his lips. "A natural ability such as yours is wasted—and *dangerous*—if left unchecked on the streets. We cannot risk that kind of exposure. You understand?"

I did. Ever since our kind left the dying lands of Emeris and arrived here, we'd been persecuted. Bordeaux. Salem. London. It didn't matter where we were. If they thought there was magic in our veins, they burned us. Buried us. Or let us starve.

Thousands of us were killed because of human ignorance. But that was a long time ago. Before cell phones, social media, and Twilight. Don't get me wrong, I wasn't exactly keen to risk it either, but I understood why some of our kind believed it was time to 'come out' to our human neighbors.

"I understand."

"Good."

"I can't go back, then? To… to where I was?"

His forehead creased. "I'm afraid that isn't possible."

Kalzir, then. I could already feel it—the cold bite of iron shackles on my wrists and ankles. The oppressive weight of the bindstone woven through the walls of my cell, supressing my magic, slowly driving me to madness.

I watched him from the corner of my eye as he gathered a quill, ink, and a sheet of parchment. My mind wandering, not quite settling on any one thing. My body light. Gaze blurred.

The metal quill-tip bit into the ink, coming out coated in the shimmery black substance. In a state of total disbelief, I read the words as he wrote them, *For Headmaster Sterling*, and then I watched as they disappeared into the paper, seeming to evaporate before my very eyes. Unbothered, he continued writing his letter, the words vanishing seconds after being written.

"Have you heard of Arcane Arts Academy?" he asked, pausing the scratching of metal on paper to glance up at me, a small smile pulling at the corner of his thin lips.

Of course, I had. How could I not? Arcane Arts Academy was a school hidden deep in the Allegheny Mountains of… West Virginia, I thought. A place for the children of great and wealthy witches to study. To develop, grow, and *hone* their natural abilities without the prying eyes of humans.

In other words—no place for a girl like me. A vagabond without a home or a penny to her name had absolutely no place within the hallowed halls of AAA.

He couldn't be serious.

"Are you surprised?" he asked, continuing before I could pick my jaw up off the floor and attempt to formulate a response. "You're welcome."

Thank you? He really wanted me to say *thank you?* They'd eat me alive in a place like that. Spoiled rich kids. Know-it-all teachers. Curfews. *Exams.* I wouldn't last a damned day. "But how long will I have to stay there?" I began, trying to keep the sour taste in my mouth from tainting my words. "Is this your *sentence* for what I did?"

"If you choose to see it that way, then I suppose it is. And I expect you to stay there until formal graduation."

AAA students graduated at twenty-one... he expected me to stay there for *four* years! Students there started at sixteen, how would I ever catch up? My mouth went suddenly dry.

I'd rather he sent me to Kalzir.

"I'll have someone escort you to gather your things, we'll have you there by nightfall."

My things? Did he mean my one lousy suitcase

of clothes and headbands? Or my hairbrush and toothbrush. It didn't matter because I wouldn't be going back to Leo and Lara's caravan. If I did, I might get out of going to AAA, but they'd be sitting where I am, and in much deeper shit. I couldn't imagine what the consequence would be for their 'negligence,' but I knew it would be far worse than the fate that awaited me.

I shook my head, letting the tension in my shoulders release. "There's no need," I told him. "This is all I have."

He clucked his tongue, his gaze roving over my tank top, torn jean shorts, and frayed headband with a look somewhere between distaste and pity. "Very well."

He sent me through the portal alone.

I turned to watch it close behind me, the old man nodding to me as the portal evaporated, leaving me staring at cream colored wallpaper.

"Yes, what is it?" A throaty bellow called from the other side of the room. I spun, tripping over a chair to land sprawled face-first on the plush oriental rug. My palms burned where they scraped across the carpet. I clutched them to my chest, finding the skin red and raw.

Damn. I jumped to my feet, a violent blush blooming red in my cheeks. Inflaming my chest.

"I'm sorry," I said, brushing invisible dust off my knees to avoid meeting Headmaster Sterling's heavy stare. "I'm sorry if I disturbed you. I was sent by—"

"I know who sent you, and I know why you're here," he interrupted, and my jaw flexed, holding in a retort. "Is there something of interest on the carpet, or are you being purposefully rude?"

I bit my lip and raised my head.

The man before me was regal looking in a pinstripe tweed suit, with salt and pepper hair, thick black brows, and a shocking silvery white beard that climbed up the sides of his face to meet his hairline at his temples. His eyes were dark and wide as they took me in. The crinkles at their corners stretched with the motion.

His lips parted, and my instant reaction was to look away. Look anywhere but at the man staring at me like I was a ghost, or maybe a monster.

Headmaster Sterling schooled his features back into something more like a drawn scowl, leaving me to wonder what it was he saw that made him startle. But then again, why wouldn't someone of his stature look at someone like me with anything but mild shock? As if they don't know the state of the world outside their plush office chairs, warm stone hearths, and fine fabrics.

Ignorance really was bliss, wasn't it?

Sterling lifted a sheet of paper from his desk,

handing it out to me while reading something else in front of him.

"Generally, if I hold something out for someone, it means it's for that person."

"Oh," I said, breaking out of my trance-like state and scurrying over to pull it from his calloused, ink-stained fingers. "Thank you."

I moved back away from the desk, peering at what looked to be a schedule of classes. Potions. Incantations. History. Alchemical Science.

"Your dorm room number is at the top," he said. "That'll be all."

I nodded, finding where he'd written the number 427 in the top corner of the page.

I supposed I'd be made to find my own way around, then.

Moving toward the door, I froze in place when he added. "And Harper…"

I didn't dare turn around, afraid I'd lose my nerve.

"I don't want any trouble from you. Is that understood?"

"Yes, Headmaster Sterling."

"Good."

I rushed out the door, gasping when my body collided with another, and I fell hard on the tile floor. Pain shot up through my tailbone to leave stars dancing in my peripherals.

I moaned, trying to stand. Noticing I'd scattered the papers of the person I'd hit all over the floor. What was *wrong* with me? Why couldn't I ever stay on my own damned feet?

Clumsiness really was a curse.

Forgetting the dull ache now radiating up from my backside, I rushed to pick up the documents, muttering an apology to scuffed brown leather shoes.

"I'm so sorry, I didn't mean to—I mean, I just wasn't paying attention—"

I cut myself off. Not wanting to sound even more pathetic than I probably looked. I clamped my mouth shut, holding my breath——my cheeks inflaming with mortification.

Could this day get any *worse?*

"It was an accident," he said, crouching down in his navy slacks and vest, tossing his loose burgundy tie over his shoulder. "Here, give those to me. Are you alright?"

I pushed the papers into his waiting grasp, sucking a breath through clenched teeth when his fingertips brushed the back of my hand. He tucked his reclaimed papers beneath his arm and offered me his hand. His grip was warm and firm as he helped me to stand.

A jolt ran through me, like a static shock, but

stronger, racing through my veins, shooting sparks from my nerve-endings.

He watched me with a curious gleam in his eyes. Eyes the color of dark denim, or the sky just before a storm. A whisper of scruff defined his already strong jaw. Full lips perched, smirking, above a dimpled chin.

His jaw tightened and his eyebrows pulled together. I watched as his adams apple bobbed.

I snapped my jaw shut, releasing the hand I didn't realize I was still holding and resisted the urge to check if I was drooling or if I'd managed to keep it all in.

Had he felt it, too?

Like calls to like, Lara's voice whispered in my mind, *magic to magic.*

I blinked rapidly, shaking my head to clear the phantom voice still ringing in my ears.

He tilted his head and the dying light from the tall stained-glass window at the end of the enormous hallway hit his face—setting his light brown hair ablaze with streaks of copper and something close to gold.

Damn… he was the most beautiful thing I'd ever seen.

Another charged moment of silence passed before I realize I still hadn't answered his question.

"Fine," I blurted at the same time he almost

imperceptibly shook his head and said. "I'm Elias. Elias Fitzgerald."

Say something. Don't just stand there!

"Harper," I choked out, composing myself. Painfully aware of how I must look in comparison to his vest and tie. With my ratty attire and messy mane of hair.

The man named Elias tucked his papers into a neat bundle. "You must be new," he said, his gaze lazily roving over my less than proper clothes, settling on my flip-flops before finding my face again.

"Is it that obvious?"

He snort-chuckled, nodding, and his expression was so unguarded. Not filled with judgment, or pity, or condescension like all the other stares I'd had to endure that day. I let out a small laugh, surprised to find I remembered how to smile.

"Do you need help finding anything?"

Right. I still had the now-crumpled time-table in my hand. "Actually, yeah. Could you point me toward the female dorms?"

"Ah," he said, looking slightly deflated. "Yes. Of course. I'm headed that way if you want a half-assed tour?"

"I'd like that."

Elias spun around as though trying to remember where he was. I wondered if he was new here, too. "Right, so, you know where the Headmaster's office is—obviously. Did you portal in?"

"Yeah. Right into Headmaster Sterling's office. I haven't seen anything else."

"Well this is the west wing of the academy. Faculty rooms and living quarters are down there," he said, pointing back the way he'd come. "Student dorms are in the east wing. And all the space in between are classrooms."

We started down the hallway, and I made a point to look around, trying to find the exits and lavatories. You know, the important stuff. But there were no exits here, instead I found walls of wood and stone. Painted portraits of Headmasters with their familiars. One with a crow. Another with a… *mountain lion?* Now that was badass. I wondered who he was.

"So, where are you from?" Elias asked, blowing out a breath.

I shoved my hands into my pockets. "No where, really," I finally answered, not really sure what else to say. "But I came here from New Orleans."

"Ah," he said, cutting me an approving glance. "I love New Orleans this time of year," he slowed, his gaze settling on my near-bare feet again. "I hope you have some proper shoes. It's a lot colder in West Virginia than it is in the south in April. And the mountains have their own weather. It snowed just a couple weeks ago."

I cringed. *Ugh,* another thing to look forward to.

We passed through a main atrium, lit by an impressive crystal chandelier that seemed to float in midair. The light was near blinding if you stared at it too long. From the atrium, which I gathered to be the heart of the building, four hallways broke off, forming the main arteries of the academy. Each labeled with their direction. North, East, South, and West.

I scrunched my face, stopping in the middle of the room. Elias' footsteps still echoing around us. "Where is everyone?"

It occurred to me then we hadn't seen, heard, or run into anyone else yet.

He gestured to the hallway marked *North.* "They'll all still be in the dining hall," he told me, and I thought I could hear the faint sounds of laughter, music, and chatter drifting from the hall. "Have you eaten?"

"Yes," I lied, not wanting to go anywhere near the *dining hall* in the prestigious AAA while in rubber sandals and a baggy tank top.

Elias seemed to sense the lie, his lips pressing into a thin line before he started off down the corridor marked *East.* I wondered why he wasn't in the dining hall eating with everyone else, but thought it best not to ask. I didn't want to seem nosey.

I walked a little ways behind him, making a show of trying to catch up to his lengthy strides when really I was marveling at his broad shoulders and the way he walked tall, without even a hint of slouch. He seemed a little older than I thought the students would look. But then again, I supposed they did attend until they were twenty-one.

"That's Ms. Granger's classroom to the right," he said, pointing out a wide wooden door. "Incantations."

"And what's in that room?" I asked him, pointing to another down the hall and to the left.

"History," he replied.

As we neared the end of the hall, he stopped, pointing up a flight of stone stairs to the right of the dead-end in the corridor. "Female dorms are up to the right," he said. "And male dorms on the left," he continued, pointing up a staircase opposite the one he stood beside.

I expected to find a bunch of elitist types in the academy. You know, the kind of people who looked down on someone like me. Looking at Elias as a small smile quirked up at the corner of his mouth, I considered the possibility that I'd been wrong.

"See you tomorrow."

He turned and walked away, leaving me to call after him awkwardly. "Thank you, Elias!"

Elias hesitated, almost turning back, before he ducked into a classroom, closing the door firmly behind him.

Heaving a long, exaggerated sigh, I hauled my tired feet up the never-ending stairs. Nearly out of breath by the time I reached the top. I vowed for the umpteenth time to get myself into less pitiful shape.

427. I scoured the hundred doorways and narrow inlets and halls. Counted through numbers that didn't seem to have any logical ascending or descending pattern. Instead the numbers were scattered about. There was 345 right next to 501, and 200 just around the corner from 111. It was madness.

After what could have easily been a half hour of grumbling through the labyrinth of rooms, I finally found it. I checked and double-checked the now-smudged room number in the corner of the page. Yes, this was definitely it.

I shouldered open the door, assaulted by the sickly sweet smell of perfume and the smooth crisp scent of clean cotton.

The room was larger than expected but I guess anything looked big when compared to the back of an old caravan, or a two-man tent.

It was easier to tell which side of the room

belonged to me. It was bare, gray, and a little sad looking. The other side of the room on the other hand had several pieces of artwork, modern, hanging haphazardly all over the wall. The bed was covered in a fluffy pink duvet and way too many pillows.

At the end of the bed pushed against the wall was an old white vanity, restored and painted with what looked to be gold foil. Moving closer, I saw its surface was littered with expensive looking creams and make-up. And tucked in the sides of the ornate mirror above were pictures of a pretty blonde girl with warm, sparkling brown eyes and a winning smile. Pictures of her and her friends and other people who I assumed were her family—including two golden-haired little brothers.

The girl I was meant to share my room with seemed to be the popular type—but on closer inspection, I found that none of the pictures were taken at the Academy. At least not that I could tell. I wondered if her popularity in the human world transferred over to AAA...

I'd never really had *friends*. Leo and Lara would say I was an *old soul* and always seemed more comfortable around adults than children my own age. And besides, when you moved around as much as we did it was impossible to make any lasting relationships.

I turned back to my own side of the room. Crisp white sheets and a threadbare plaid throw blanket were neatly folded at the end of the worn-looking mattress. A small nightstand with a single drawer squatted to the left of it, and above that perched a small window in the rough stone wall of the exterior of the building.

I went over to get a look outside and found the ground over thirty feet below.

The grounds were well kept, with flagstone trails snaking around the academy and what looked to be a garden off to the right. But beyond the borders of the grounds there was nothing but forest. Peaks even higher than the one the academy sat on reached for the sky off in the distance.

Sunset cast an ominous orange glow over the scene, and the only sounds to be heard were birdsong and the chirping of crickets. Even I had to admit it was beautiful in a haunting sort of way.

Blowing out a breath, I spun to find a polished navy steamer-style trunk sitting at the end of my bed that I hadn't noticed before. On top was a heavy looking piece of cardstock paper with one word scrawled across the front, *Harper.*

Strange, I thought.

No one else knew I was here, did they? I lifted the notecard, flipping it over to see there was a sentence written on the other side.

These should get you started. Good luck.
    C.W.

I remembered seeing the very same initials on a nameplate atop the Council delegate's desk. But what could he possibly have sent me? And why was he so keen to try to 'help' me?

Discarding the note onto my bed, I unlatched the top of the trunk and heaved it open. My nose wrinkled at the musty smell inside. But its contents were far from being old or worn. It was all brand-new.

Neatly folded in the trunk was an Arcane Arts Academy uniform. A stack of blouses, all embroidered with the triple A emblem of the school on the breast. Below them was a kilt-like skirt or two, a couple of navy colored blazers, one burgundy red sweater, and two sleeveless pullover vest things.

Digging toward the bottom I also found a pair of simple white tennis sneakers, undergarments, and even a toothbrush, toothpaste, and a bore bristled hair brush with what looked like a hunk of *bone* for a handle.

Great… everything a budding witch needed… just missing the pointy hat and broomstick…

I huffed a half-hearted laugh, dropped the things back inside, and let the lid fall shut.

With a groan, I kicked off my flip-flops and fell

onto the mattress, the springs creaking and groaning in protest to my weight. The metal coils poked into my ribcage.

My eyelids felt instantly heavy, and I struggled to hold them up. I couldn't remember ever being so completely exhausted in my entire life.

4

———

A clattering sound had my eyes snapping open. Immediately closing them again when they were assaulted by white morning light.

Moaning into my pillow, I turned my head slowly, squinting into the room and remembering all at once everything that had happened the day before. I was not on my tiny sleeping mat in the back of Leo and Lara's caravan, nor were we in one of the dusty motel rooms we sometimes stayed in as a sort of treat.

My guardians would know by now where I was. They likely did a locator spell to figure it out. But even though I asked them not to come looking for me, I was a little surprised to find that they really hadn't.

They were probably happy for me. I could

picture them—staring in mild surprise at the spot on the map where the scryer would've landed. Looking at each other with a mix of shock and relief.

They would think I was lucky to be sent to a place as renowned and prestigious as the academy. The fact that I was here was probably the only reason they didn't come after me... afraid to ruin my chance to study in the only academy for witches in the United States of America.

I'd have to find a way to get a message to them. To explain it wasn't my fault, and that I was sorry. *Soon,* I told myself.

Another clatter had me rubbing the sleep out of my eyes, dragging my tired and aching bones into a halfway sitting up position. Was she *trying* to wake me up? No one made that much noise unless it was on purpose.

A pair of eyes the color of steeped tea stared at me through the mirror above the vanity across the room. One perfectly plucked eyebrow raised and two rows of straight white teeth smiled. The girl set down her powder brush, turning to me with a face only half made up.

"Oh, hi!" she chirped, sitting up and rushing over to introduce herself.

I pushed myself the rest of the way up and swung my legs over to put my feet on the ground, hissing when the soles of my feet connected with ice-cold tile. She shook my hand, buzzing with positive energy. There *had* to be coffee somewhere in here. No one woke up with that much energy in the morning.

"I'm Bianca," she said, cocking her head while doing some sort of little curtsey thing. "When my uncle told me I was *finally* getting a roommate, I could hardly believe it. I mean, it's been great having a whole room to myself for a full *year*, but this is going to be so much more fun!" The girl clasped her hands together, practically bouncing with excitement. Her soft blonde curls bounced with her.

"Oh, I'm so rude," she continued, her brows pulling inward. "I forgot what he said your name was. I would've asked you myself, but you were out cold when I came in from dinner, and—"

"It's Harper."

"What?"

"My name. It's Harper," I answered her, brushing the hair away from my face. "Who's your uncle?"

"Headmaster Sterling," she said like it was the most *obvious* thing in the world, biting her bottom lip as though suddenly nervous.

Suppressing the urge to roll my eyes, I flopped back onto the bed. Great, the headmaster of the academy totally put me with his niece on purpose. *He must have.* Probably to keep tabs on me. I wondered if she volunteered, or if she even knew she was his spy.

Bianca's expression darkened for a moment, a drawn look glazing over her eyes before she blinked and pasted a smile back on her face. She went back to her vanity and sat down hard on the cushioned stool in front of it. Bianca continued blathering on about something, but I wasn't really paying attention anymore.

A fat white rabbit with long, floppy ears and beady red eyes stared at me from atop her pillow across the room. Its tiny nose twitched as it watched me, looking wholly unimpressed by what it saw. I swallowed. It was obviously her familiar. There was no other reason for her to have an animal in her dorm room. It wore a little silver collar around it's neck, and squinting, I thought the heart-shaped name-tag said *Blanche.* It was fitting, I supposed.

"… but then he said that you were new and you didn't even have a familiar yet, or all that much experience so it would be good if you roomed with someone like me who…"

Where were earplugs when you needed them? My head throbbed as if I'd spent the night digging into Lara's wine stash instead of passed out by seven o'clock. I shoved aside the embarrassed flush attempting to take root and fester in my chest. Like I needed to be reminded that I was seventeen and *still* hadn't found my familiar.

Rising from the bed if only to escape Bianca's endless chatter, I dug through the trunk at the end of it, pulling out simple black slacks, a white blouse, and the cozy looking burgundy sweater. Grabbing the bone-handled hairbrush and toothbrush as an afterthought.

"Bianca, was it?" I asked, interrupting her spiel about how great her uncle is. "Can you tell me where the showers are? I didn't see them last night."

There were no other doors in our dorm room except for the one I entered the night before to come in, so obviously there was no bathroom in here—which meant bathrooms would be shared. But in all my wandering trying to find the elusive room 427 I hadn't seen anything that looked even remotely like a lavatory.

"Oh, there's no time for that! Class starts in fifteen minutes."

She must've seen the panic in my eyes because she turned and said, "Sorry, I guess I should've woken you sooner," with a sour look on her face and caught her bottom lip between her teeth again.

I dropped the clothes onto my bed and lifted the brush to my tangle of red hair, mumbling *crap, crap, crap*, under my breath.

Dragging the brush through the knots with one hand, I dug around in the covers for my lost headband with the other, finding it lodged near the bottom corner of the bed.

Fifteen minutes. Alright. That's not that bad. No time for a shower, but I could still manage not to look like a total bum, right?

Turning, I caught my reflection in Bianca's mirror. Gasping at what I saw.

Christmas incarnate… It was Leo's very apt description of me. He said it one Christmas when I was just a kid, and the nickname stuck. I saw that fiery little girl again now. A mass of long wavy vermillion locks framing an ivory face and large bright green eyes.

Maybe it was cute when I was a kid, but now my eyes were bloodshot, and my skin just looked pale and sallow. There wasn't time to fix it, not if I wanted to be able to at least *pee* before going to class.

Grateful I still had a hair elastic around my left wrist, I pulled my hair into submission, winding it into a round messy bun on top of my head. Then I pulled the headband into place to hold it all together. It would be the best I could do without a good heavy-duty conditioner.

Snatching up my clothes, I rushed behind a privacy screen to dress. Stripping off my baggy tank top and ratty shorts.

"What class do you have first?" Bianca called from the other side of the screen.

"History."

Or at least that's what I thought the timetable had said.

"Me too!"

Convenient.

I wondered if her uncle had anything to do with that, too. I was willing to bet our timetables probably shared several similarities.

Bianca dutifully waited for me to finish getting ready, hopping from one foot to the other by the door. The bell rang, sounding more like an air-raid siren than an alert to make your way to class.

I could tell Bianca was resisting the urge to tell me to hurry up. She looked like she was in pain. Her pretty made-up face was pinched. As soon as I stood from tying my new shoes, we flew out the door and through the hallways.

There were a few other stragglers meandering their way to class, and I was grateful none seemed to notice the new girl being near-dragged down the stairs. I assumed Bianca was a student who was *never* late for class. How could she be? The niece of the academy's headmaster, no—I was certain she would be expected to make a good example for the other students.

The thought had me thinking maybe I was

wrong about her. Maybe, like me, she was forced to play a role she didn't ask for, and to wear a smile while she played it.

But then again, she could also be one of those self-appointed class president types. Happy to do as Uncle Sterling asked and spy on her new roommate. Time would tell.

We hit the bottom step as the second bell sounded, my bladder protesting not having been able to relieve itself.

Bianca shuddered at the siren that meant she was officially late.

I sucked in a breath. I supposed I had slept through breakfast as well since Bianca pulled me straight into a classroom filled with students. The door closed behind us all on its own.

Bianca dropped my hand and ran to take a seat at the front of the class. *Shocker.*

There was only one other empty seat—at the very back in the right-hand corner.

I kept my head down, trying not to pay any attention to the soft whispers and stares of the other students in the classroom as I walked quickly past them to the back. Knowing it would be best not to hear what they said.

Try as I might to block them all out, it was impossible not to notice how the other girls looked.

Hair gleaming, with flawless skin and wrinkle free blouses.

Privileged was the only way to describe them. They'd probably scream if they knew they attended the same school as someone who regularly shopped in thrift stores and ate hot dogs from carts in the street. Maybe they'd petition to have me expelled…

Now *there* was an idea.

Taking my seat in the back, I peeked up from under my lashes, noticing how the guys' uniforms were almost the exact same as the girls.

And none of them wore a deep burgundy tie like Elias had the day before.

Skimming through the bodies in the classroom, I considered the backs of several of the male students' heads before deciding, no, Elias was *not* in this class. They all seemed too young. He must have been in one of the fourth or fifth year classes. *Damn.* It would've been nice to see a friendly face.

As though he'd read my thought and come to the rescue, the door swung back open and he strolled in. His head bent as he studied something on a clipboard. His thick hair flopped down over one eye.

I beamed at him, ready to wave him over to sit next to me once he looked up, but then…

"Good morning, Mr. Fitzgerald," Bianca said,

and I saw the corner of the sweet smile she threw him as she turned her head.

Elias nodded to her, setting down the clipboard he had been studying on the desk at the front of the class. He removed a worn leather satchel from his shoulder and inclined his head to her. "Miss. Matthews."

No.

Hell *no.*

A shiny new nameplate sat at the front end of his desk facing all the students.

ELIAS FITZGERALD

Professor of Arcane History

My throat went dry.

Mr. Fitzgerald lifted his gaze to regard the rest of the classroom. "Good morning, class."

A few of the other students returned his greeting, though most remained quiet, pulling out notebooks, and textbooks, and pencils from their desks. I heaved a sigh when I found my own desk contained the same things and I wouldn't have to ask *Mr. Fitzgerald* for them.

I shifted in my seat, trying to sink below the heads of the students in front of me.

Of course, he found me anyway. His haughty stare hesitated on me for an instant before he cleared his throat and went back to taking documents out from his briefcase to start the day's lessons.

A teacher? Really?

I crossed my arms, wishing the floor would open up and swallow me whole.

Just my luck.

5

———

By the time lunch finally rolled around I was *starving*.

My stomach was in knots, and I almost walked into a wall on the way to the dining hall, eliciting a string of giggles from a trio of girls as they strolled past me in their shortened kilts.

When was the last time I'd eaten? I tried to rack my brain for the answer, but the last meal I could consciously remember eating was breakfast yesterday morning. *Before* the whole fiasco with the jewelry thief.

The mouth-watering aromas of hearty chicken soup, fresh cucumbers, and roast beef wafted down the hallway, propelling me to go faster. All thoughts of handsome teachers and annoying roommates and classroom screw-ups vanished from my mind. I had one single focus.

Food.

Stumbling through the double doors, I found the hall to be *enormous* with high ceilings and tall stained-glass windows stretching from floor to ceiling along the far wall. Depictions of the various phases of the moon arched over a beautiful garden scene cast in hues of blue and purple.

Tables laden with all manner of food and drink stood in front of a pass-through window that I assumed led to some sort of cafeteria kitchen.

If it weren't for the ache of starvation in my gut, I could've marveled at the beauty of it all day. Instead, I ran to join the line of students forming on the left side of the table.

An older woman in an apron shoved a big oval-shaped plate into my hands, a scowl on her face, when a flash of blonde hair caught the light and I found Bianca off to the right of the windows at the other side of the room. The afternoon sunlight captured the gold tones in her hair, and made her creamy skin gleam like polished ivory.

I almost called out to her, hopeful for one second that I wouldn't have to sit alone. But then I saw him. Headmaster Sterling stood next to her, partially concealed in the shadows next to the column of light entering through the windows.

He seemed to be watching me. His gaze flicked from his niece, back to me, and to her again.

Already reporting on all the things I'd screwed up that day I was sure. My stomach dropped, and I scooped a giant portion of mac and cheese onto my plate.

Oh well… there really wasn't anything I could do about it. Maybe the more I screwed up the more he wouldn't want me around. Maybe the headmaster was the perfect person to find a way to get me out of this prison sentence. From the looks he had given me the night before, and the one he'd just given me now, I didn't think he wanted me here any more than I wanted to be here.

Though I had to admit, I'd already learned a good deal in the half a day of classes—even if I did have a bit of trouble concentrating on anything other than Elias in Arcane History, and had my brain turned inside out in Alchemical Sciences.

After filling my plate with more food than I could reasonably fit in my stomach on any given day, I scurried to an empty smaller table near the windows *far* away from Bianca and Sterling. At least I'd have something to look at that wasn't all the eyes in the room staring at me.

I ate in silence, and just as I'd known would happen, no one dared approach my table. Not even Bianca. In fact, the seats from the neighboring tables closest to me also remained vacant. You'd think I had been infected with some sort of plague and they were afraid of catching it.

More's the better. I didn't want to be friends with any of these people, anyway.

I popped another handful of grapes in my mouth, near-moaning at the sweet, cool liquid as it slithered its way down my throat.

Elias entered the dining hall a moment later. I tried not to look, but I couldn't help it.

He raised his hand slightly as if to wave but dropped it to his side a split second later. I blushed and looked away quickly, a sour taste making me lose what was left of my appetite.

W HEN LESSONS for the day ended, I finally felt like I could breathe. Then I remembered I had to do it all over again tomorrow. And the day after that.

And the day after that.

But I had to thank whatever gods were out there that none of the teachers in the classes I'd had to endure that day forced me to introduce myself. I had no idea what I would've said. *Uh, hi, I'm Harper. Nope—no last name. Let's see... well, I've been living out of the back of a caravan selling illegal potions to mortals since I was a toddler. Oh! And I've never been to a real school,* and

I accidentally split open the French Quarter yesterday. Nice to meet you all…

Yeah, because that would go over *so* well.

But of course, that didn't mean I managed to escape notice entirely.

In true Harper fashion, the potion I tried to brew in the second class of the morning exploded all over my sweater even though I would've sworn I had followed that recipe to a T.

And in incantations I smashed my head on the ceiling while trying to levitate—I still had the bump to prove it.

And then just when I thought the day was starting to turn around, I almost stepped on Professor Granger's familiar, a ferret, in sigil's 101. At least she hadn't made a big deal about it. And even snapped at the other students to hush their snickering.

She'd seemed nice. Not like the other teachers— well save for Elias. But he didn't count since I was still having trouble believing he was a history professor and not a student.

Not in the mood to run into him again, or Bianca, or Headmaster Sterling, I rushed to the dining hall at dinner hour and swiped a few rolls from the top of a bread basket before taking off back to my dorm room. But it was too sad and lonely in there, so I pulled on one of the navy blazers from the old steamer trunk, stuffed the rolls deep into its pockets, and went to find my way outside.

Where it was nearly impossible to find my way around inside of the academy, it seemed exceedingly simple to find my way out. As though I already knew the way.

Bottom of the stairs, down the hall—*run* past the history room, turn down the southern hallway, past a huge looking library that I would have to check out later, and there it was, the way out.

And with everyone still at dinner, I really didn't think anybody had seen me. *Double bonus.* I crept down the thick stone staircase into the slight chill of the evening. There wasn't another soul in sight, and for the first time in almost two days I took an unrestricted breath. No one to watch me trip over my own feet, or mess up a simple spell, or stare at me with judgy eyes. Just me, the sky, and the ground beneath my feet.

I pulled one of the bread rolls out of my pocket and tore off a chunk of it with my teeth, savoring the yeasty buttery flavor and set off down the narrow path away from the academy and into the woods.

It didn't take long before my thoughts wandered

back to the academy and consequently to *Professor* Fitzgerald.

Stop it, Harper. You can't have him. He's a teacher.

Get over it.

But there had been a connection, hadn't there? And why didn't he say he was a teacher from the start? He totally led me to believe that he was a student. How was I supposed to know?

The thin trail I was following wound away from the grounds and into the woods. Through small clearings and copses of trees. A canopy of newly budding leaves above and a damp carpet of earth below. The air had that musty scent of wet wood and young plants that signified the start of spring, but a chill still clung to the air.

Turning back, I could just make out the top spires of the academy through the trees.

As the sun fell lower, about ready to dip below the horizon, I thought I should probably turn back.

But… what if I didn't? If I just kept walking…

There had to be a town somewhere around here. I didn't think anyone had seen me leave. Maybe they wouldn't find me. Maybe they wouldn't even look.

So, I kept walking, telling myself I wouldn't go too much further, when in fact I wasn't even sure if I would stop at all. After what could've been a few minutes or maybe closer to twenty, the sky darkened, the temperature dropped, and a shiver ran up my spine. And was that *mist* rolling down from the north?

The forest had come alive with sounds. The rustle of twigs and leaves. The sound of bugs chirping and buzzing. *Beautiful,* I thought. *But also eerie as hell…*

And then a howl.

I stopped, my body going rigid at the ear-splitting cry. So close. *Too* close. Another howl rose to meet the first, and I took a step back, catching my tennis shoe on a tree root and falling backwards onto wet dirt. My gaze darted through the trees and the underbrush looking for the telltale glow of yellow eyes. But I saw nothing, and the howling stopped.

Shadows played with the remaining light in the forest, tricking my eyes. The mist made it impossible to see clearly. My heart beat erratically in a chest now coated in a fine layer of cold sweat and the hair on the back of my arms and neck prickled.

Idiot, I thought, trying to shake some of the muck and dead leaves off my palms. What was I thinking?

Just get back to the academy. Walk slow, I told myself, *try not to make too much noise.*

I pushed myself back to my feet and spun,

freezing in place. My hands shot out in front of me —fingers splayed, stiff as a corpse.

The gigantic wolf snarled. Its hackles were raised, and its mouth was dripping with steaming saliva. It beared its teeth to me in a feral growl.

"Good dog," I said, my voice hitched and broken. "That's it… it's all right. I won't hurt you if you don't hurt me, okay."

Think, Harper. Use your magic. Your brain. Anything. Do something!

And then I did the thing they tell you not to do when faced with a wild animal instead—I looked it square in the face.

Our eyes locked together. And then I felt it.

My heart beat once, hard. Air slammed deep into my lungs and then a sensation like something clicking into place, settling in my bones and rippling through my body.

The wolf cried out, recoiling as though struck. Whimpering, it bowed its head to the ground. Making sounds so pitiful and so pained that I had to resist the urge to go to it. To console it.

Just as the wolf began to recover from whatever was happening to it, another wolf came soaring over a tall bush, landing forcefully in front of the other, sliding—its claws dragging in the dirt from the force of the impact. The second wolf growled, snapping at me before it lunged to attack. I screamed, raising my arms to shield my face.

But just before its hind legs left the earth to go straight for my jugular, our eyes met between my wrists and it happened again.

The beast let out a high-pitched yip before it barreled into me, tucking his head down and turning his body. The wolf's torso knocked into my chest and I went soaring through the air before skidding to a stop in the dirt, my arms taking the brunt of the impact from wrist to elbow. Burning, stinging, and slick with more than mud.

Quick as I could I flipped over, finding the wolf whimpering not more than five feet away from where I laid against the ground. My heart did that strange beat thing again, except this time it was almost agony. I whimpered, crying out. Unlike the last time, this time there was a gut-wrenching tearing sensation, like my heart was being cleaved in two, before the pieces clicked in and I was left dazed and gasping for breath

"It's alright," I whispered through shuddering breaths, reaching out to my familiars with hands covered in decaying foliage and blood.

I heard the *thump thump, thump thump* of feet pounding against earth and turned just in time to see him fly out of nowhere to land in a crouch right in front of me.

He threw up a ward around us, its rippling, shimmery surface created a strong barrier between Elias and I and my familiars. The wolves, startled by his entry and still reeling from the force of the bond, turned tail and sped off back into the mist.

They'd be back. Familiars couldn't stay away from the witch they were bonded to for long. But still, he'd scared them, and I'd already done enough of that.

"What did you do that for?" I whined at Elias, wincing as I attempted to stand from the ground.

He knelt down in the mud before me, lifting my chin to the light of the dying sun to look into my eyes. I stiffened.

"You're bleeding," he said, lifting my hand from the earth to examine my scraped forearm. "You shouldn't be out here all alone. The woods are no place for a young witch at night."

"What? Is this the part where you give me detention?" I snapped, pulling my hand away.

Elias recoiled, his eyes darkening as he moved to stand, not responding.

"Where'd they go?" I asked, looking through the dense trees for any sign of them as I begrudgingly took Elias' hand to help me get up. "My familiars… why did they run away?"

"Your what?"

"The wolves. I felt it. The witch familiar bond,"

I paused before I told him the other part, unsure if I should omit it—not knowing how it was possible or what it meant. But then, like always, I blurted it out anyway. "With *both* of them."

Elias shook his head, dropping my hand with an incredulous look in his eyes. There was tension in the set of his jaw and in the way his lips were pressed together in a thin line. "Those weren't wolves, Harper. They were Endurans."

The word hung in the air between us.

Impossible.

There weren't any shifters in these woods, were there? They couldn't have been. A witch couldn't bond to a shifter. I'd never heard of such a thing.

My skin crawled at the idea. I really hoped he was wrong, but something deep down told me he wasn't. Shifters and witches did *not* get along, but then again, none of the other species really got along with us. We had the mistakes of our ancestors to thank for that. They'd cut out the tongues of the Vocari people in Emeris, slain thousands of Fae in Meloran, and then to top it all off, they'd been the cause of the curse on the Enduran and Vocari people.

It didn't matter that it had been nearly a thousand years since then; immortals tended to hold grudges.

"We'll talk after. Let's get you cleaned up and inside, it's freezing out here."

I hadn't realized I was shivering until he laid his own suit jacket over top of my blazer, his hands rubbing warmth back into my arms as he guided me slowly down the thin trail back toward the academy.

6

───────

I thought he was leading me back to the academy, but just as I started to be able to see bits and pieces of it through the trees and we were fully in its shadow, Elias veered off, leading us down another trail.

"Where—" I had been about to ask where he was taking me when I saw the darkened shape of what looked to be a tiny cabin nestled in a grove of bushy pine trees.

"These are my quarters. Do you mind? If you go back to the academy now, with mud in your hair and cuts and scrapes all down your arms…" he trailed off. He didn't need to say anymore.

If anyone saw me, I'd surely be sent to Headmaster Sterling's office. Made to answer for why I was alone in the woods and what happened. Would he even believe me? Would anyone when I told them I'd bonded to *two* Enduran shifters in the woods?

But the more important question at the forefront of my mind was… would Elias tell anyone if I asked him not to?

I was enough of a pariah as it was. Already an outcast among the outcasts. There had to be a way to undo it. To sever the bond. And if there was, I'd find it.

Swallowing past a lump in my throat and licking my dry lips I answered. "No, it's fine. Thank you." We climbed the three steps to the small front door, a faint orange glow coming from the window to the right.

The hinges let loose a stuttering groan when Elias pushed the door open, gently herding me inside, looking back over his shoulder as he did. My head just fit through the top of the doorframe, but Elias had to hunch over to keep from smashing his.

I got why he was so tense though… I supposed it wouldn't look right for him to have a student in his quarters.

Inside the small cottage-like cabin a fire burned in the hearth. Mostly embers now. Elias rushed to grab a log from the basket beside it, tossing it in. It was dim aside from the glow of firelight and smelled like him. Like warm spice and cold mountain pine. With only a hint of the mothball scent that came inevitably with the age of the cabin.

It was sort of like a studio apartment, or a motel room. A small kitchenette occupied the space to the right of the hearth, along with a wrought-iron two-person bistro style table covered in tomes, notes, and other documents.

"Sit down," Elias said, hanging an old-fashioned kettle over the fire, which had devoured the log and grown several inches in height. I could feel the light touch of its warmth on my shins and sighed.

Elias muttered to himself as he dug around in a dresser at the end of a double bed covered in rumpled blankets and lumpy pillows. I jumped when I noticed two yellow eyes staring at me from under the bed frame. And then the creature slinked out, its ears and tail erect as it sniffed the air.

It was a silver fox. Though it was more deep gray and black then it was truly silver. Only the very tips of its ears and tail bearing the trademark metallic color of its name.

It came to me slowly, creeping over with silent steps.

"Hello," I whispered, and the fox's hackles raised, and it made a strange strangled sound before it skittered back under the bed.

"Don't take it personally," Elias said, pulling

what looked like a small first-aid kit out of his bottom drawer. "He doesn't like anyone."

He came to kneel in front of me, holding a hand out for my injured arms. "I'm just going to clean out the dirt, and then we can use a healing sigil to do the rest, okay?" he asked in a voice like velvet that managed to be deep and gruff, while also being soft and seductively warm. I'd have let him do whatever the hell wanted to me right then.

I nodded numbly. The moment his steady hands took hold of my arm, grasping it gently in the place just above my elbow, I melted and froze all at once. The calm he radiated seemed to penetrate the aura of shock, fear, and worry that felt near closing in. Dismantling it from the inside out.

He made quick work of my forearms, his hands deftly working to clean the dirt and muck out of the many tiny lacerations. He didn't speak while he did it, just worked quietly, his jaw tense and brows drawn.

When the shock had almost completely worn off, and the warmth of the fire reached bone depth, the tension left my body. I slumped into the unforgiving iron of the chair, suddenly lightheaded and exhausted.

"I'm sorry if I hurt you," Elias said, drawing the sigil over my forearms that would help speed the healing process. The simple glowing circle and cross symbol seeped into my skin, making it glow too, and tingle for a moment before the magic of the sigil faded and the lacerations began to close. The process was slow, but they'd be healed within the hour instead of within days.

Being a witch did have its perks.

"I hardly felt it," I said, blowing out a breath.

A beat of uncomfortable silence lingered between us before I started to feel awkward and like I was imposing.

"I really should go," I said, dropping his suit jacket on the back of the chair as I stood.

Elias' large hand closed around my wrist. "Wait," he implored me, swallowing before he added, "Are you certain you bonded with them?"

"I am."

The connection I'd felt to the two wolves in the forest was undeniable. Leo and Lara had always told me I would know when I'd found my familiar, but I didn't think it would feel quite like it did. They didn't say anything about it being so painful.

Regardless, I was completely certain. It didn't matter that I thought it was impossible because it had happened. To me.

"It doesn't make any sense," Elias said, more to himself.

I huffed. "You're telling me."

His hand still circled my wrist, and with him so

close, I could've sworn I could hear his heart beating. Loud and fast, but steady. His warm spice scent mingled with the smoky tang of burning wood, dragging a sigh from my lips and a shiver from my body.

How could he not feel that?

My magic awakened within me, buzzing in my veins as it came to life. It nudged my senses into overdrive and ignited a fire deep in my belly. The wild tendrils of it reached out from my core, tentatively stroking at the cage of my skin as if attempting to reach out to the man standing before me.

He had to feel it too. He *had* to.

"Sorry," he said in a rush, letting me go to rub a palm against the scruff on his chin. He turned away before sitting down hard in the opposite chair at the table.

"For what?"

"I didn't know you had bonded to them… I just —I heard you scream when I was on my way to the academy for dinner. I knew it was you," he said, raising his head from where it was hung over spread knees to find my face. "I don't know how I knew, but I just did. I wouldn't have stepped in if I'd known."

I didn't forgive him out loud. He had done the right thing. He knew it as surely as I did. There was no way he could've known.

Because no one had ever bonded with a shifter before, or any of the other species either. We were bound to animals, not shifters, or vamps, or fae.

"What do I do?" I asked, my eyes pricking and chin quivering.

Without taking his eyes off me, Elias wove his fingers together at his front. "Don't tell anyone."

My stomach dropped. I was sure my shock at his suggestion showed because he hurried to explain what he meant.

"The bond may have somehow been superficial. Or maybe, it won't forcibly draw you together like a normal bond between a witch and an animal would."

Normal bond.

I clenched my hands into fists.

"You don't know that," I argued, my voice laced with exasperation and something like rage.

Elias shook his head. "Neither do you."

Wait, why was I arguing? Wasn't this what I wanted? For him to agree not to tell anyone?

He went to grab the kettle from the fire, bringing it over to the countertop to pour into a little brass teapot filled with loose-leaf tea. Earl Gray if my nose didn't fool me.

"Did you know that I'm new on the faculty?"

Elias set the teapot and two cups on top of the

mess of papers coating the table between us, gesturing for me to sit back down.

I shook my head, wanting to tell him that I didn't care he was new. And ask him why that mattered right now.

"The last history professor who worked here died at the end of last term. Heart attack, I think it was. Anyway, I had already made something of a name for myself in the community because of my thesis on witch evolution—and the evolution of the other species. But really it boiled down to a case of me being in the right place at the right time. It was Sterling himself who offered me the job."

I cocked my head at him, sitting to take the tea he offered me.

"So, are you saying you think my magic is more evolved… or that the shifters have somehow changed?"

He curled two fingers into the handle of his mug, holding it tightly but not raising it to take a sip. "I don't know, but either option is possible. And I'm probably the only person at the academy who would believe you."

"So?"

"So," he repeated, taking a long drink of his tea. "I have a proposition for you. I won't tell anyone about what happened in the woods if you promise to come straight to me if or when they come looking for you."

He leaned in close. "Come to me and only me." His storm cloud eyes practically burned a hole through me with their quiet intensity. "Do we have a deal?"

BIANCA WAS UP STUDYING when I got back that evening. She looked up from her notes with a worried expression, her hair still damp from the shower.

I mumbled to her that I lost track of time studying in the library and needed to rush to get washed up before bed. I didn't give her time to respond or to look too closely at me before I snagged a towel without asking and ran out the door.

The lavatories were the only part of the old castle-like building that seemed to have been upgraded. When I entered, I was surprised to find newer looking plumbing and more modern stainless-steel fixtures. Large oval mirrors formed a perfect line over a bank of raised bowl sinks. There were eight shower stalls on either side of the wide room, closed off with thin white curtains.

A few toilet stalls ran along the back wall, and benches formed a half-moon shape in the middle.

The floors were wide terra-cotta tiles. And it was windowless. Steamy. The smells of fancy soaps mingled with the stagnant mildew smell of floors in a perpetual state of wetness. The air was humid from the mad rush to shower before lights out, but at least it was warm.

It reminded me of the bathrooms at the campgrounds we often stayed at—granted this one was a *bit* nicer. Not for the first time that day, a black mood fell over me at the thought of my guardians. I wished they were here with me. But getting upset because they weren't wouldn't help. They'd *freak* if they knew what'd just happened to me in the woods.

I shivered. The cold from outside had made a home in my chest and tissues. I was afraid not even a hot shower would help me be rid of it.

There were only a few girls left, and they sat applying creams to their faces and brushing their hair, perched on the benches like pretty little birds.

They grew silent when they saw me, and I'd rushed into one of the curtained stalls, praying none had looked too closely. There was definitely still mud caked into my hair. My slacks were covered in dirt, and the scrapes on my forearms still hadn't fully healed.

I felt like the bond I'd made with the two shifters in the woods was somehow written on my skin. Like if anyone looked too closely, they'd just know or smell it on me or something.

I've always been a shit liar. And even more terrible at keeping secrets.

So, when Bianca was oddly quiet the following morning, which was super out of character for her... I couldn't help thinking she somehow knew where I'd been. Could somehow feel I wasn't being honest. It was driving me insane.

She kept glancing up at me through the mirror on her vanity, her eyes narrowed, a thoughtful, if not slightly confused look on her otherwise serene face. I thought maybe she was waiting for me to say something. To start a conversation. But she would be waiting a very long time for that. I was afraid to open my mouth for fear all of my secrets would come pouring out and I wouldn't be fast enough to shove them all back in.

I hadn't had time to brush my hair when I returned from the showers the night before, the lights blinked out not more than a few seconds after I'd re-entered the room. At least the dark and the late hour gave me an excuse to not have to hold a conversation with Bianca, but it had made getting into my pajamas and into bed super difficult. I'd stubbed my toe twice before I finally found safety beneath the covers.

After sleeping with damp hair washed with

crummy shampoo and watery conditioner, brushing it was a nightmare and took nearly twenty minutes. Finally, I managed to get it to an acceptable level of neatness and pulled my head-band into place. The wondered when I'd stop having to regret cutting bangs into my hair last year…

Bianca's creepy rabbit stared at me from atop her pillow, its pinkish red eyes seeming to almost glow. Its little whiskers twitched.

"Does it always stare at people like that?"

"Maybe Blanche knows she's rooming with a liar, too."

And there it was.

"What are you—"

Bianca turned on her cushioned stool and glared at me. "You weren't in the library last night. You lied."

"How would—"

"Because I was in the library."

I finished lacing my shoe, pulling the knot tight before I stood to square my shoulders at her. Scowling through the mad blush crawling up my neck. "So, what? Going to run and tell your uncle, then?"

She made an ugly snarling face that managed to somehow also be hurt before she threw down her wide toothed ivory comb. "Is that what you think?"

she snapped, mumbling something that sounded suspiciously like a curse word under her breath.

"It's what everyone thinks! Always the same," she mumbled, gathering up a pink notebook and a fluffy white pen. "Headmaster Sterling this, Uncle Sterling that. Bullshit."

And then she stormed out, leaving me standing there dumbfounded.

I groaned when the morning bell assaulted my ears and I remembered history was my first class of the morning.

It wasn't fair, I mused, pursing my lips from my seat at the back of the classroom. Having to watch him from his untouchable spot at the blackboard.

The sun decided to show up to work today, heating the academy through the many tall windows, creating a sort of greenhouse effect that left the air hazy and just a bit too warm for comfort. I was sure there was a spell, or sigil, or some sort of incantation they generally used to cool it. Some sort of witchy air conditioning.

But I was glad whoever was in charge of doing that hadn't gotten around to it yet. Elias—*er*—*Mr. Fitzgerald* had removed his suit jacket, and I couldn't help but notice the top button of his crisp white dress shirt was undone, showing off smooth tanned skin at the shallow dip of his collarbone. He didn't look to be sweating at all. Which was so unfair.

Even though I'd put on the weird kilt-like skirt that morning and had opted for a short sleeve blouse, I was *still* sweating.

I brushed the hair from my neck, trying and failing to stare at what he was writing on the board instead of at him.

The sleeves of his dress shirt were rolled up to his elbows, settling in the crease there. His biceps—I didn't think I'd paid enough attention to them before.

What a mistake that was.

The thin white cotton material was stretched taut against the bulge of his arms, making him look more like a bodybuilder than a teacher.

I licked my lips, suddenly wishing I'd stopped for a glass of water before class. One of these days I'd wake up in time for breakfast.

My mouth was so dry.

It's so damned hot in here.

"Harper?" Elias said, pointing at something he'd written on the board. And I got the feeling it wasn't the first time he'd said my name.

"Sorry I... I didn't hear you. What was the question?"

The trio of girls sitting two rows up giggled. The

one with the pin-straight yellow hair turned in her seat to raise an eyebrow at me, snorting.

Bitches.

Elias cut the three girls a warning look, and they immediately faced front, their fingers clasped elegantly on the wooden surfaces of their desks.

So, I wasn't the only one to have a crush on Elias Fitzgerald then...

Quickly, I skimmed what was written on the board in Elias' neat handwriting.

My jaw clamped shut at what I found, my toes curling in. Maybe it was because of what happened the night before, and maybe it wasn't. But I was sure Elias sensed I didn't know much about shifters... since I hadn't even picked up on what they were before he told me.

Either way, it seemed today's lesson would be about the Enduran race.

"What can you tell me about the Enduran race prior to the curse that made Emeris uninhabitable?"

Several sets of eyes in the classroom turned, awaiting my response. Waiting for me to mess up or say the wrong thing. And I wouldn't disappoint them.

Living among gypsy-like vagabonds and humans my entire life made my knowledge in the subjects of ancient immortal history and things like alchemical science almost nil.

What do *you know?* I asked myself, flailing around in my mind for some semblance of an acceptable response.

I knew that before the curse infected the land of Emeris and the people on it, vampires were just Vocari—a race of people who could compel the thoughts and actions of others through speech. And shifters were known as Endurans. A warrior race blessed with uncommon strength and speed. But I didn't really know much else.

"Well, they were one of the three races on Emeris—before the curse made the immortal land uninhabitable. They were strong and fast, but they weren't ruled by the moon, and they weren't yet able to shift."

Elias nodded, his deep blue eyes showing approval. "Very good, thank you."

He turned to the rest of the class. "And what can the rest of you tell me about how the Enduran race has changed since then?"

The yellow-haired girl piped up, raising her hand, but not waiting for permission to speak. "They're more impulsive," she offered, a note of distaste in her nasally voice. "They're known to be a small-minded sort of people. Unable to control their urges to shift in the presence of a full moon."

"In your opinion, Kendra, they're a lesser

species," Elias responded. Not so much a question as it was a statement.

The guy sitting in front of Kendra leaned back in his chair. "The curse made the Endurans slaves to the moon, and made the Vocari unable to walk in sunlight," he said, turning to wink at Kendra. "It made them into beasts—monsters. They're more like animals than people."

Elias looked disappointed, and I wondered if he was thinking the same thing I was. Neither of the other students had acknowledged the role the alchemist race—*our race*—had played in making them the way they are today.

If it weren't for what our ancestors did, the other two races of Emeris wouldn't be cursed.

There wouldn't be this animosity between races.

Who knew where we'd be then? Maybe we'd all still be back on Emeris. The land might not have fallen into plague and darkness. Maybe when the Vocari took back the throne all those years ago, they'd have ruled peacefully.

Perhaps our races would've someday found a way to put aside our differences. To live and work together toward a better future.

But we'd never know. Time-travel was the most forbidden form of magic there was. And even the knowledge of it and *how* to do it was locked up in the original Codex. Lost, or maybe destroyed? I couldn't remember. But I knew the Codex, and all the original alchemical texts it contained, were gone.

"Yeah," the girl named Kendra said. "Everyone knows that."

My brows raised, and a lick of disgust made me flinch. They were so naïve. So holier-than-thou and all that bullshit. If they took just *one second* to step down off their high horses, they'd see we were the ones who had behaved more like animals. Or at least, our ancestors sure as hell did.

There were many different beliefs among our kind. Some thought themselves better than the other races and looked down on them as though they were animals, or bugs, to be squashed under polished leather boots. That same group also thought of humans in a similar light. It was why the Council had forbidden witches to take mortal lovers. Well, that and something else about impure bloodlines in the future of our kind.

There were others, too, who lived a magic-free life. A sort of penance for what our ancestors did.

The last sect was the most radical. All of them were of a resolute mind that all races should *come out* to humans. That we should make ourselves known to them and stop living a life in hiding among the shadows. They thought we should fully integrate with the humans and protect them from the other races.

In a way it did make sense. We could never go back to our immortal homeland. It was dead and gone. And the only other land shrouded from view by humans was inhabited by Fae, and we weren't welcome there either.

Our ancestors burnt *all* the damned bridges.

So, it was the mortal lands or bust.

Over the last near one thousand years we'd done our best to make a home for ourselves here, but that last sect of witches believed that a home could never be a home if you had to hide in it.

I didn't really care either way. But if I was being honest, I didn't really trust humans either.

As the rest of the class nodded or voiced their agreement with the yellow haired Kendra and the buff-looking jock dude, it was easy to guess which sect made up the majority of the academy. Not surprising.

Elitist pricks.

"I think it's sort of beautiful," Bianca said into the stagnant air, eliciting a few gasps from the other students, and gaining herself the full attention of Mr. Fitzgerald.

She fidgeted in her seat, suddenly uncomfortable under the scrutiny of the rest of the witches in attendance. "I mean," she continued, floundering. "Wouldn't it be cool to turn into a wolf?"

"No," Kendra said, her top lip curling back over freshly whitened teeth. "Why would anyone want to turn into a stupid, flea covered dog? *Gross*."

Bianca's shoulders slumped, and even though she didn't turn around, I saw the red stain of an embarrassed blush working its way up the back of her neck. I watched as she fisted her hands beneath her desk.

"Why don't you tell us, Kendra?" I blurted. "Since the only *bitch* I see in here is you."

The class collectively held its breath. Buff jock guy whistled low between his teeth, and Kendra looked near ready to implode as she rose from her desk and turned to face me, staring down at me with bared teeth. "You better watch yourself new girl—"

I was sure she was about to go off on some sort of tirade about how she was so important and how I was so, well… *not*. But she was saved from having to waste her precious time by the bell, and I was saved from having to listen to her crap.

"That's enough," Elias called to us over the sound of rustling papers and chairs scraping against the floor as the other students rose to leave, taking their time as they went—probably waiting to see what Kendra would do.

But Elias came to rest a hand on her shaking

shoulder, and she spun, doing that hair flip thing that only popular girls managed to pull off before she stormed from the classroom.

I collected my notebook and shoved the history textbook back into the desk. I'd almost made it to the door and freedom when two words froze me in place.

"A word," Elias said, stuffing his hands into the pockets of his navy slacks.

The two girls who I assumed were like tumors on the hips of Kendra paused on their way out to give me a look that told me without the need for words I now and forever would be labeled as a loser. It was kind of a Catch-22 wasn't it? That only the winners got to decide who the losers were.

With a flick of his fingers, Elias closed the door behind the other students, and with a speedily drawn sigil he pulled a ward up from the earth, making it so no one outside of the door could hear what we said inside.

"Look," I said, turning to face him. "I'm sorry, but that girl deserved—"

"I don't care what you said to Kendra," he replied, raising a brow at me with a slight shake of his head. "Though I wouldn't put it past her to tell Headmaster Sterling, or at the very least to make your life at the academy a little less agreeable while you're here."

Right, because it's been *so agreeable* so far.

"Then what?"

He sat down at the desk nearest him, lounging in the stiff-backed wooden chair as though it were the most comfortable thing in the world.

Looking so out of place.

I don't know how I ever thought he was a student.

He regarded me with contemplative, guarded eyes. "I saw them again last night—the Enduran shifters."

He brought his steepled hands to his face, resting his two index fingers against his lips as he considered what to say next. "They were sniffing around my cabin. I think they caught your scent there."

So, they'd come looking for me already. The whole thing was so confusing. I didn't know what to do. Should I go looking for them? Introduce myself…?

Bonding with an animal was supposed to be easy. Familiars protected their witch counterparts as they came into their powers and acted as a sort of magical battery—lending strength and power when the witch was in need of it. Every witch bonded to a familiar. There were no exceptions.

Some took longer than others to find their animal counterpart, but most found theirs within the first year of coming into their powers.

I came into my powers nearly *three* years ago.

Familiars stayed with their witch until death. And, of course, witches took care of their familiar animals as best they could. Prolonging their short lives so they could remain with their bonded witch for as long as they should live.

Familiars were made to be irrevocably loyal and trustworthy. Their love unconditional. The bond unbreakable.

But the wolves I'd bonded to in the woods were not simple animals. They also had humanoid forms. And the human mind was a treacherous thing. People lied, stole, backstabbed, and manipulated. People did things animals would never do.

People were dangerous.

I sank into a chair opposite Elias, most of the frustration and anger I'd felt at Kendra only moments before disintegrating. "What should we do?"

Elias's eyebrows raised at my question, and a finger of heat traced a straight line up the back of my neck when I realized I'd said *we* in reference to a problem that was really only mine.

He sat very still, moving only his lips when he said. "We—"

"I didn't mean to imply that—"

"*We*," he said again, more strongly. "Don't do anything yet. I can't be certain what their intentions are, but Harper… I don't think they were looking to say hello, if you know what I mean."

I cocked my head at him, not quite sure I understood.

"Fallon, my familiar—well, from the way he was acting when they were near… if they know what happened—that they'd been bonded to you, they may be looking for their own way to sever the bond."

I shivered, the truth of what he was trying to tell me in as gentle of a way as he could becoming clear.

My familiars were out for my blood.

I didn't know why I was so surprised. Of course, they'd kill me if they knew it meant severing the magic tying us together.

"Hey," he said, brushing a strand of hair back from my forehead. "We can't be sure of anything yet. I don't want you to worry. We'll figure this out."

His fingertips lingered near my jaw, and I could still feel the ghost of them along my temple. I blinked rapidly, trying to quell the delicious sensation dancing along the surface of my skin.

We, I liked the sound of the word when it came from his lips.

He went back to the front of the classroom, and I went back to breathing normally, not realizing I had stopped.

Clearing my throat, I gathered up my things from the desk, realizing I was more than a little late for my next class and hoping there wouldn't be some form of punishment waiting for me there.

"I'll look into the possibility of severing the bond," Elias said, beginning to erase the day's lessons from the blackboard. "I've never heard of it being done before," he continued, pausing in his work to give me a sympathetic glance as I hovered near the door. "But that could be because no one's ever needed such a spell. Granger might know something, or there may be texts on it in the library."

I nodded numbly, knowing he was only trying to make me feel better. Little did he know that I'd been waiting *years* to bond with my familiar.

Moving from place to place, with no familial ties and no true friends. I'd always thought when I finally found my familiar, I'd have at least one constant companion in my life.

And now my only option was to sever that bond. Even though we both knew you only bonded to a familiar once. If Elias somehow found a way to do it, I'd never have a familiar.

I walked from the classroom without another word, wishing more than anything that I could go crawl back into my bed and stay there.

8

___

*I*t'd been three days since I'd seen the shifters in the woods.

I hadn't seen them since, and neither had Elias. And we hadn't really gotten an opportunity to talk much since the other day after class. What little communicating we did was mostly done in a series of different looks, nods, mouthed words, and shaken heads.

It gave me a sort of thrill—if I was being honest. The two of us working together in secret.

But he still hadn't found anything on severing the bond, and the not knowing, and the not having a plan, had me on edge and twitchy.

Elias warned me to stay indoors until he figured out a solution, but tomorrow marked the start of outdoor phys-ed. In the near week it'd been since I arrived, the winter chill left the mountain, and spring could be felt in warm ribbons on the wind.

It would be fine. Two shifters wouldn't dare approach an entire class of witches, not to mention the more experienced teacher who taught the class as well. Elias was a bit more skeptical, but eventually agreed.

"Late again, Harper," Ms. Granger said. "Once more and I'll have no choice but to give you detention."

"Yes, Ms. Granger. Sorry about that."

I rushed inside to the sound of her familiar, Frankie—the moody ferret—hissing at me from his makeshift bed of paper atop Ms. Granger's desk.

There was only one open spot left, and it was right beside Bianca at the two person high-top desk. Sigil's 101 was a standing class. Granger believed that since our magic was derived from the earth, feet planted firmly on the ground and an erect spine would make for easier practice.

All I knew was every time I left her class it was with sore feet and a tired mind.

Sigils were a form of advanced magic. And could be used to create portals, heal wounds, grow stuff, to strengthen or weaken. I once saw Lara use a sigil to kill every mosquito in a few miles' radius… I hadn't even known there was a sigil for that. There really was a way to do almost anything with magic.

Incantations were used to strengthen the power of sigils or perform simple spells—like, say, changing the color of your hair, or turning lake-water to lemonade. And potions were more science-based. I likened them to baking. You had to follow the recipe exactly or the potion, elixir, or compound simply wouldn't do what it was supposed to. Potions were a very volatile form of magic—and consequently the most difficult for me to master.

I was what Leo would call a 'natural witch'. Where most witches had only a small amount of natural power and used things like sigils, incantations, or potions to strengthen their ability, I had the opposite problem. When trying to strengthen the raw energy drawn up through the earth into my veins, something almost always went haywire.

Some of the most renowned witches in history could create massive storms, turn a person to ash where they stood, and even create objects from nothing. But I was willing to bet they didn't do any of that by accident…

"Hey," I whispered to Bianca as I slid into my spot beside her at the tall desk.

Her bubblegum pink lips pursed, and she didn't raise her eyes to meet mine. So, we still weren't speaking to each other. Awesome. I had done my best to avoid her the last few days, scouring book after book in the library to try to find a solution to my little wolf problem—only going back to the dorm room in time for lights out.

She spent an inordinate amount of time in the library too, but at least it was large enough that we could be on opposite sides and not be within sight or earshot of each other.

It was starting to get awkward though. And tense, and a little annoying.

As Ms. Granger went on about proper sigil formation and its crucial importance because of all the different variants and types of sigils, I leaned in a little closer to Bianca's side.

"Are you really going to stay mad at me forever? I said I was sorry."

"Yeah, but not sorry enough to tell me where you *actually* were."

I rolled my eyes. "Look, Bianca, I'm sorry that your uncle is Headmaster Sterling. That must really suck," I said, and I meant it. I saw him wandering through the library, his gaze falling on me way more than what would've been normal. And in the cafeteria. And in the hallways. He seemed like he was always watching me. She had to understand that I couldn't trust her to keep secrets from her own flesh and blood.

"Can we just," I started. "I mean, I'd like to just start over."

Bianca dutifully scribbled copies of the sigils Ms.

Granger was drawing on the board, but I could tell she was considering my offer. It would be nice to have one friend in this foreign place. And Bianca was not the bimbo I had originally thought she was. Like me, she'd been forced into wearing a mask she never asked for.

"I promise," I said, waiting for her to look at me. "If I could tell you where I was, then I would. But trust me when I say you don't want to know."

"Something you'd like to share with the class, Harper?" Ms. Granger trilled, turning from the board with one hand on her hip and the other poised over the blackboard with a nub of chalk.

I shook my head. "No, sorry."

Biting the inside of my cheek to stifle the discomfort and the blush trying to crawl into my cheeks, I set to doing my work. Ferociously, I scratched the sigils into my notebook to catch up to everyone else in the class.

"Fine," Bianca said after a time, and I noticed some of the tension in her neck and shoulders had relaxed. "We can start over… and I'm sorry."

I scrunched my eyebrows at her.

"It really wasn't any of my business where you were. I just—I just *hate* being lied to."

I nodded, both to her and to myself. Of course, she did. Who didn't? I could understand that at the very least. "Okay, no more lies then."

She nodded back. "All right. Then we start over."

Stifling a small smirk, I went back to trying to catch up. My smile faded into a grimace as I beheld the chicken scratch on my pages as compared to the beautiful swooping lines and swirls on Bianca's.

I had a lot of work to do.

By the time the end of class rolled around my stomach was growling and my fingers and wrist were cramped. We hadn't done any actual practicing of sigils. Only studied how to draw them and watched Ms. Granger perform a few of the simpler ones.

"Harper," Mrs. Granger called out from the front as we packed our things. "A quick word if you don't mind."

Bianca gave me a tight-lipped smile and a small shake of her head before she whispered. "See you in the dining hall," and sauntered out of the room with the rest of the class.

I readjusted my headband, tucking the hairs that had liberated themselves back in before I made my way to the front of the class. "If this is about me being late, I promise it won't happen again."

Ms. Granger finished up writing something down on a piece of parchment. Her long wavy brown hair lit with streaks of bronze and gold fell forward to cover her face. When she looked up, I found she had warm brown eyes, set in a gently long face with full pale lips, and a strong chin.

A younger version of her could've had a career in modeling, but age had crinkled the skin around her eyes and mouth. Lucky for her, the wrinkles only gave her more character, and added a sort of homey mother-like feel to her features.

"I should hope not," she said with a knowing smile, straightening and spinning in her chair to get a better look at me. "But I only asked you to stay behind to see how you're doing."

My eyes narrowed with something like confusion, or maybe it was suspicion. But there was no condescension in her tone, and her gaze held nothing but curiosity, and maybe a little bit of empathy, too.

Swallowing past a sudden lump in my throat, I clutched my notebook and pen tighter to my chest. "Well, I—I've never been to a real school before. It's… quite a lot more difficult than I imagined it would be."

Ms. Granger nodded her understanding, though I really didn't know if she did understand. If anyone at this place could. All the teachers and students at Arcane Arts Academy came from wealthy families and dignified backgrounds.

But the fact that she was even trying gave me a little bit of hope.

"I thought so," she said knowingly. "Which is why I wanted to extend my help. If there's anything you aren't understanding, or anything that needs clarification, please do feel free to come to me once classes are finished for the day."

I was taken aback by her offer. Elias aside, every other teacher in the academy had been standoffish and harsh toward me. I wasn't sure if everyone knew the circumstances that led me to be a student here, but either way, the teachers weren't willing to cut me any slack.

And as though my past and lack of position in alchemical society were written in permanent ink on my skin, they regarded me with disdain. Making me a leper before I even had a chance to prove otherwise.

I wondered if it had something to do with the fact that Ms. Granger was the only female professor within the academy. Where the rest of the world seemed to be moving into the direction of true equality between genders, the witching society had a long way to go before they caught up.

"Thank you," I said, and truly meant it.

"It's no bother," she said, and my grip on my notebook lessened. The shiny gold of my father's ring caught the light, reflecting it into Ms. Granger's eyes.

I watched as her mouth slackened, and her eyes

widened before her hand snaked out and she snatched my hand, pulling me toward her roughly.

Her shoulders shook. Her hands were near vibrating where they still clutched mine. I tried to pull my hand away, making a sort of weak squealing sound between my lips.

Snapping out of her strange state, Ms. Granger finally let go of my hand and I stumbled two steps back. "Where did you get that ring?" she asked, rising from her seat, her hands clenching into white knuckled fists.

"Did you steal it?" she almost yelled, taking a step closer. Her warm brown eyes lost all of their gentleness. Her full lips puckered into the epitome of bitch-face.

"No," I gasped, stumbling further backwards until my back met the closed-door. Did she recognize the ring? How?

"Harper," she warned, her jaw clenching and eyes gleaming in the bright fluorescent lights of the classroom.

I held my one hand and my notebook up in a placating gesture, my heart racing. "I didn't steal it, I swear. It—it belonged to my father."

You would think I'd stuck her with a cattle prod —the way her entire body went rigid, her lips parted, and her brows raised so high they nearly disappeared into her hairline.

Then just as quickly, her shoulders sagged, and her hands unclenched.

"That's impossible," she said quietly to herself.

I resisted the urge to run out of the classroom and tear down the hallways—to get as far away from the woman who was staring at me like I was either a monster or a ghost as I could. But I was too stunned, and I'll admit more than a little curious to do much more than stand there.

"Oh!" she breathed, her hands flying up to cover her mouth. Her gaze devoured me from my toes to the top of my head. "Oh," she gasped again. "You are their child."

My lungs felt near giving out, along with my knees. *She knew them.* She knew my parents. My palms grew clammy, and a fevered sweat broke out over my chest and the back of my neck. I'd never met anyone who knew who they were.

I never knew anyone who could tell me a single thing about them.

My hope that I wasn't wrong was so strong I was near shaking with it. Buzzing with impatience. Waiting to be disappointed.

I didn't dare speak, afraid to ruin everything. I was afraid if I opened my mouth, she would suddenly turn around and say she was mistaken, and she never knew them at all.

But she didn't do that.

"I don't know how I didn't see it before. You have his eyes…" she said softly, her voice breaking near the end. "And her red hair."

I couldn't believe it. I was stunned. Stupefied. I had about a million questions. Suddenly, hunger was the last thing on my mind. I didn't care about shifters in the woods. Or insanely hot history professors. "You… you knew them?"

Ms. Granger dropped her hands slowly to her sides and stepped back to lean on the edge of her desk. "I knew your father," she replied, still analyzing each one of my features. "Where have you been all this time?"

I stiffened, the air freezing in my lungs. I had been dreading that question for nearly a week, but now answering it didn't seem so bad. At least not answering it for someone who might understand it wasn't my fault how I'd lived the last seventeen years of my life.

"Traveling from place to place," I told her, swallowing back the urge to lie. "I—I never really had a home. Not since…" I trailed off, unable to voice the fact that my father died, and my mother abandoned me as a baby.

Ms. Granger looked confused. "I'm sorry about your father," she said, eyes downcast, clutching at the ledge of her desk for support. "But what about your mother? You haven't been with her?"

Steeling myself against the rising swell of ugly emotions in my core, I said in a deadpan voice. "She abandoned me when I was very small."

"No," she said, shuffling her feet against the floor. "That doesn't sound like her. Not to say that I knew her very well, but I'd assumed she'd gone into hiding. I always thought she would've taken you with her."

Apparently not.

"You look so much like him," she breathed, a glazed look of nostalgia in her eyes.

Not that I was any sort of expert on the subject, but by the way she spoke, and the inflection in her voice, and the antsy body language every time she mentioned him, I thought maybe she had been more than friends with him. Maybe she had loved him.

"Will you tell me about him?" I asked her, a burning sensation clawing its way up my throat. Moving very slowly, and trying to keep my breathing steady, I settled myself down into one of the desks near the door, hiding my shaking hands between my knees.

"I'd love to," she responded with a faraway look. She sighed fondly, waving a hand gently through the air. "Where to begin..."

9

———

I was ecstatic and brooding all at the same time during the next day's phys-ed training. I couldn't stop thinking about what Ms. Granger told me about my father. Alistair Hawkins. Which made me Harper Hawkins.

I smiled through the pain as we ran laps around the academy. It wasn't bothering me at all how far behind everyone else I was. *Harper Hawkins.* I liked it. But it felt strange and foreign on my tongue. Having gone so long without a last name it was super awkward to suddenly assume one.

I wondered if they'd update my file at the academy or if the teachers would start calling me Miss. Hawkins instead of just plain old *Harper*. I'd never assumed Leo and Lara's last name, and they'd never forced me to take it. Just thinking about them made me feel guilty. I still hadn't had a free second to find a way to contact them. They would be sick with worry by now.

I'd kill for one of our quiet nights by the campfire. The pacifying sounds of Lara's guitar lulling me to sleep.

Ms. Granger told me a good deal about my father before it became too late and she had to get back to grading papers and I had to get to the dining hall before they shut down for the evening. I learned that my father went to this very same academy with Granger when they were both younger.

She told me he was a brilliant mind and a powerful witch.

I wasn't surprised.

She told me his familiar had been a wolverine, and I'd stared at her in wonder. I never heard of someone having a wolverine as a familiar before.

But then again, I never heard of having two Enduran shifters as familiars either…

Like father like daughter?

It became more and more obvious that Granger had had more than just friendly feelings for my father by the way she spoke of him, and how sad and forlorn she seemed when remembering he was gone.

If I was being completely honest—I was jealous.

I wished I'd had the chance to know him, but now I never would. All I would ever know was what I heard through the stories of others. I had to admit, though, it was more than I had before.

But there was one thing about what she'd said that was bothering me. She told me she assumed my mother went into hiding. But why would she need to hide? I mean, I knew witch and human relationships were frowned upon, but the Council wouldn't have punished her. The worst they would have done would've been to erase her memory of my father being a witch, and all associated memories.

Isn't that what she wanted? To forget?

Isn't that why she abandoned me all those years ago?

Bianca came out of nowhere, falling into stride next to me. I nearly tripped over a raised piece of flagstone but managed to maintain my balance, stumbling back into a jog.

"Hey," she said, and I couldn't help but notice how she wasn't even close to out of breath yet. "I missed you at dinner last night."

After a quick bite, I'd snuck off to take a shower and didn't make it back to our shared room until after lights out. Thank goodness I'd remembered the sigil for illuminating dark places or I never would have found our door.

"I was in Granger's class for a while," I replied,

and suddenly the need to tell someone about what I discovered overwhelmed me. "She knew my dad," I blurted through labored pants. And then I realized I hadn't really told Bianca all that much about myself. Where I knew she had two younger brothers, and that Headmaster Sterling was her uncle—she knew almost nothing about me. Because that's how I'd wanted it.

"I—I never got a chance to meet him. He died when I was just a baby, and my mom left after that."

If I was going to try this whole friend thing, it would probably help if she knew who I was.

The soles of our shoes slapped the flagstone pass in unison, and I watched as Bianca's face contorted before she recovered her composure and waited for a few of the other runners to pass before she responded.

Kendra tossed us a dirty look over her shoulder as she passed. Her familiar, a beady-eyed crow, cawed sharply at us from above. "Both my parents are gone, too," she said once Kendra was out of earshot. "They died when I was eight. My uncle is my guardian now."

But I had seen the photographs of her parents, and of her and her friends… pictures taken when she was younger. I could be so daft sometimes.

I judged her before I even knew her. Maybe we did have a little more in common than I thought.

"I'm sorry."

Bianca shook her head, her light blonde ponytail bobbing at the back of her head. Her hair somehow still managed to shine even though the sky was horribly overcast and a dull shade of gray.

There was no sign of the sun anywhere. In fact, it looked like it might rain. I wondered if that would get us out of running laps, or if they'd make us do it anyway. "At least I got to know my parents before they passed," she offered.

True.

"And the little boys I saw in the pictures in our room?"

She smiled a little at the mention of them. "They're with the nanny full-time," she said with a half-smile. "But I get to visit them sometimes on weekends. I'm actually going to see them tomorrow."

Weekends?

"Does everyone get to leave campus on weekends?"

Bianca shrugged. "If they want. A lot of them portal home, but some stay back here to study."

The weekend was tomorrow. But, without a parental guardian on the outside, I'd never be allowed to leave.

I groaned inwardly, sighing my frustration.

"Guess you don't get to leave, huh? You don't

even have, like, guardians that can sign you out or something?" A note of pity had crept into her voice, but when I dared a glance at her face, I saw only empathy and understanding.

I really didn't want to lie to her again, but it wouldn't technically be a lie since Leo and Lara had never *formally* became my guardians. They were just the people who took me in.

I made a mental note to ask Elias how to do a communication spell so I could send them a message. I'd have to get outside the ward surrounding the academy to do it though. "No," I replied, near breathless from the exertion of running. "It's just me."

"I get that. Sucks, doesn't it?"

"Less talking and more running!" The phys-ed instructor shouted at us as we passed him, blowing his whistle loud enough to make my ears sting.

Bianca stopped, and I slowed to a walk beside her. "Mr. Ironside, may I be excused to use the ladies room?"

Why hadn't I thought of that?

Ironside begrudgingly nodded his assent, and Bianca turned back for only an instant to throw me a wink before she skipped off back toward the academy.

"New girl," Ironside shouted. "Get moving!"

He blew his whistle again, and I resisted the

urge to flip him the bird before speeding up ever so slightly into the slowest jog known to man.

Not more than a few moments later a ghost-like prickle stroked the back of my neck. The small hairs there stood on end. My brows pulled together, and my fingers tingled. Someone was watching me.

I whirled around, whipping my head in the direction of the trees bordering the academy grounds. It only took me a second to find them.

Two huge wolves watched me from behind the bushes. One bared its teeth, and the other snapped before it sank back, disappearing behind the leaves. A second later a sandy blonde-haired male rose from behind the bush. Naked.

I slowed, trying not to trip. My gaze darted around in front and behind me. But it seemed the rest of the class had moved on. Already around the next corner.

I stopped and stared. My pulse thrummed in my chest like the beating wings of a bird taking flight. The one in his human form looked pissed right the fuck off. Even at this distance, I could see how his gaze narrowed and his shoulder muscles flexed. And... how rock hard and tense his abs were. Damn, was that a six-pack or an eight-pack? And his skin! Perfectly tan.

If only that bush wasn't so high. A few inches

shorter and I'd be seeing a lot more than just sexy man chest.

The pull connecting us through the bond tugged at a spot just below my breastbone. The male grimaced, and I wondered if he could feel it, too.

And then as quickly as he'd shifted a moment before, he changed back into wolf form. They both stepped out from behind the brush, staring at me intently before they turned to walk slowly into the forest.

I don't know how I knew, but I just did—they wanted me to follow them.

A movie reel of myself being torn apart by giant claws and sharp fangs flashed through my mind and my toes curled inside of my tennis shoes. A sound like a whimper crept through my lips as I bounced on my feet, unsure what to do.

I would have to decide fast. The rest of the phys-ed class would be coming around the corner in less than a minute and then I wouldn't be going anywhere.

Shit!

My feet started moving before I consciously told them to do it. I'd have to trust that they would at least hear me out before going straight to the biting part. Endurans weren't inherently bad. Or small minded. No matter what bitch-face Kendra seemed to think.

If I told them I was looking for a way to sever the bond, maybe they would just leave me alone. At least for now. Until I delivered on my promise.

I gulped down my fear and smothered my anxiety in clenched fists. And then I followed them into the trees.

I knew I was getting closer when an intense feeling of relief washed over me, and my senses sharpened, as though someone had taken a whetstone to them as I walked. I pushed my shoulders back and stood straighter, not even realizing I'd been slouching, or how draining being apart from my familiars had made me.

I'd forgotten about that part.

Now that the bond had begun to form, I'd feel weakened without them near. And they'd find it physically painful to be parted from me. Yet another reason for them to want to kill me

Great.

I carefully stepped over a moss-covered log, squealing as a giant toad hopped out from under my feet. I was deep into the canopy of trees now. No one from the academy would be able to see me, but I thought if I screamed loud enough, they'd be able to hear me at least.

Almost there. I heard a strange cracking sound, and then a movement over the earth. I shoved a few branches out of the way, ducking low to avoid a thick bow. When I came up on the other side there they were.

All the oxygen left my lungs in a great *whoosh*. Not in their animal forms, the two Endurans sat atop a tall boulder. They were dressed in nothing but loose shorts. Barefoot and bare chested.

They watched me with animalistic precision as I stepped lightly out of the shadow of the tree and into the gray light filtering down through the canopy of leaves to dapple the forest floor.

This was a bad idea. I stood staring, perfectly still. Afraid moving might break the spell and they'd attack.

But how could something so beautiful be so dangerous? The two Enduran shifters sitting lazily atop the boulder, arms resting atop knees and heads cocked, could've been gods.

The one on the left had dark caramel hair and thick brows that shrouded narrow yet bright green eyes. Stubble shadowed his jawline, and his meaty shoulders narrowed to a slim, tight waist. And even though he was sitting, the length of his bent legs gave away the truth of his height. He would stand at least a head taller than me, if not more.

The other one let loose a low growl in his throat. He was the one who'd shifted before. With hair closer to blonde, and even more muscle than his friend.

I struggled to catch my breath, unsure what to do or what to say.

The blonde one jumped down from the boulder, took two quick steps toward me until we were face-to-face, and I was cowering back from him, magic shooting up from the earth into the soles of my feet, snaking out through every one of my veins. I reined it in, not wanting to start an unintentional fight.

The Enduran's muscles bulged as he flexed, and his eyes seemed to glow as he leaned in close. "I'd start talking if I were you," he snarled, a thick vein protruding out from his neck, pulsating with pent-up energy. "Give us one good reason why we shouldn't tear you apart," he roared in a deep timber, the sound reverberating around us.

I flinched.

The other man, still sitting atop the boulder, hopped down to join his friend. I had been right, he was tall. And stood towering over me. I'd never seen an Enduran this close-up before. *Hell*, I wasn't sure I'd ever seen an Enduran at all. They mostly kept to themselves. Made their homes deep in uninhabited forests.

"I…" I started, but the word stuck in my throat. I wasn't sure what to say. It was plain to see they were looking for a very specific sort of response, and I was afraid of what might happen if I didn't give them what they were after.

The taller one crossed his arms over his chest, the veins plainly visible through his skin. "Start by telling us what the hell happened. What did you do to us?"

Did they really not know?

Steeling myself against the raucous of emotion and the trembling in my knees, I swallowed, saying in the strongest voice I could. "We bonded. But—but it wasn't my fault. It's not like, well… I mean, witches—we don't have a say in in who we bond to," I said, the words spewing out in a jumbled rush.

The two men shared a look, and I caught their scent of whiskey and cedar. With an undertone of something more heady. An animal smell.

I could tell I'd confirmed their worst nightmares were true. They had already known, and were likely as unwilling to accept it as I was.

"We'll have to take you to Atlas," the one with the caramel colored hair said. "He'll know what to do."

Take me? No.

I can't let them take me anywhere.

Think Harper, think.

I bit the inside of my cheek, looking up at them. "I don't know who Atlas is, but I can tell you if he isn't a witch, he won't know what to do."

The more muscular one grabbed me by my shoulders. His fingertips stabbed into my skin.

"You're coming with us," he snapped, a furious glimmer in his eyes. Eyes, I couldn't help but notice were the color of parched summer soil, with lighter flecks that shone like sunlight through honeyed bourbon. Somewhere between brown, gold, and amber.

I let my magic radiate over the surface of my skin, careful to keep a firm hold on it. It zapped him where his hands gripped me, and I was able to wriggle out of his grasp and shove him away. He looked taken aback at my strength—or maybe he'd felt it, too—the shudder when my bare palms met his bare chest. My pulse slowed, and there was this sensation of utter relief. A meeting of souls.

I replaced the wonderment and confusion with anger at what he'd just done. Allowing venom to seep into my voice. "I am *not* going anywhere with you," I hissed, glaring at the pair of them. "I'll find a way to sever the bond. Only a witch can do it."

The one on the left barked a pained laugh. "I can think of a few other ways to sever it," he said maliciously. "But I don't relish the thought of killing you. Whatever this bond has done to us…" he trailed off. "Besides, killing you might piss off the Council and our pack doesn't need that shit." He dropped his intense stare, sighing sharply.

"Just give me time," I implored them. "And you need to stay away from the academy, if anyone else finds out what happened, I don't know what they'd do."

Not to mention, they wouldn't like shifters skulking around in the woods so close to the academy grounds.

The other one clenched his fists as he turned to look at me. "Easier said than done," he growled, never breaking eye contact with me. "We can't stay away for more than a day without some *thing* drawing us back here." He kicked a large rock and it soared through the air like a soccer ball, smashing loudly against a tree somewhere far into the woods.

"I'll find a way. It's not like I wanted this either."

Some of the tension leached out of the blonde one's shoulders and jaw. His expression softened. "We didn't think something like this was possible."

I worried the pleats of my skirt, eyes downcast. "Neither did I," I admitted. "What can I call you? My name's Harper," I added weakly, even though we were long past the point of civil introductions.

"I'm Adrian," the blonde one who was still standing mere inches in front of me said, some of the ire gone from his voice. I got the feeling Adrian was the hotheaded type. Acting first and considering the implications later. "And he's Cal," he said, jabbing a thumb in the direction of his friend.

Cal grabbed Adrian by the arm, tugging him back a few feet. "I'd rather not tell Atlas if we don't have to," he said in a low whisper, and I looked away, pretending I couldn't hear. A blush turned the sides of my face hot all the way to the tips of my ears.

I was trying not to eavesdrop, I swear... but I couldn't help it. I gathered from their clipped, hushed conversation that Atlas was their leader—or their *alpha* I guess. Watching the two Endurans argue, I suddenly wondered where they were from. They looked to be in their early twenties, if not even younger. But like the other races, they were blessed with extraordinarily long lives. Not as long as Fae lived, or vamps, but a lot longer than witches.

How far had they traveled from their pack land when they happened upon me in the woods?

It must've been far. I doubted any Endurans would purposefully live so close to a witch academy.

After a few more tense moments, the one named Adrian raised his honey amber eyes to rest a hard steady stare on me. "We'll give you a week," he said, and there was no room for argument in his tone. "Then we tell Atlas, and resort to other... methods of severing the bond."

A week. They were giving me a week to do something that to my knowledge had never been done before. But I had to find a way to do it. They hadn't said it outright, but it was certainly implied. If I didn't succeed...

I shivered at the thought.

"Agreed," I said before I could change my mind or say something stupid.

Without another word, the two Enduran males turned away. And in the same movement used to drop their shorts to the forest floor, there was a horrible snapping, popping sound—like when your spine cracks all the way from the bottom to the top, except stronger, louder. And then before I could blink the two naked men were gone, and in their place were two wolves.

One with Adrian's gold ones, and the other with Cal's green ones, like oakmoss drenched in sunlight. They were both silvery gray, but Adrian had a flick of stark white on his forehead and paws. And Cal's tail was tipped in black as though it'd been dipped in a paint bucket. They were magnificent.

They each cut me one last glance before racing off back the way they'd come, their claws turning up dirt in their wake.

They were *fast*. The fastest things I'd ever seen. And I waited until I couldn't see them—until I couldn't hear them anymore before the reality of what happened finally crashed over me and I sprinted back to the academy, feeling my body weaken and grow more sluggish with each step I took away from my familiars.

10

I didn't get more than fifteen paces before I passed through the ward. My skin bristled at the foreign magic as my body broke through. She appeared a split-second later and I couldn't slow myself down in time. We went down in a mass of bruised and tangled limbs—in plumes of blonde and red hair.

All the air was knocked from my lungs, and I wheezed. Waiting for it to return so I could scream at her. How long had she been there? What had she seen?

What had she heard?

Stupid! How hadn't I noticed she followed me? I thought she'd gone inside…

I gulped air down, gasping. After a few labored breaths the tightness in my chest began to ease.

She moaned, holding her wrist as she moved to stand back up. Her eyes shot furtive glances at me, a worried furrow pulling her brows inward. She managed to look both guilty and completely innocent at the same time. I didn't know what to think.

"What…" I said in a strained version of my voice, still trying to get air to my lungs. "The… hell… are you doing out here, Bianca!"

She gave me an impish half smile. Implored me to understand with an apologetic stare. "I saw you going into the woods alone… I—I was worried you were going to run away. I just—"

"You just what?" I practically shouted, brushing dirt and leaves off my backside as I moved to stand, my joints groaning.

"Didn't want you to leave…" she trailed off, unable to meet my eyes. "And then I saw those two guys with you and I just *knew* they were Endurans. They looked so angry and I was afraid they might hurt you. So, I stayed hidden in case— well, I don't know, in case you needed help or something."

Idiot, I thought. But an honest idiot. It was plain to see she wasn't lying. She really was just worried and trying to help.

I felt instantly deflated. She was lucky the Endurans hadn't heard her or seen her coming. I shuddered to think what they might've done.

"Did you hear us?" I asked her, a chill creeping along my shoulder blades.

She caught her bottom lip between her teeth and gnawed on the baby pink flesh. "Not really," she replied, shrugging. "But maybe I could help. Are you in some sort of trouble?"

I laughed, and the sound was shrill and broken. I laughed because, well, what else could I do? *Was I in trouble…*

She had no idea.

Bianca looked at me like I was crazy, raising her eyebrows. "Are you okay?" she asked, worry lines creasing her forehead as she reached out to place a hand on my shoulder.

My laughter quickly morphed into horrible, wracking sobs. No, I was not all right.

"Oh, Harper," she said, and tugged me into an embrace that smelled of sweet perfume and clean cotton.

BEING friends with the headmaster's niece had perks. When I finally stopped crying and we walked back onto the academy's grounds, Bianca had given the phys-ed teacher one sharp look and snapped, "I'm taking her to her room," when he tried to stop us from entering the building.

He'd sucked in a breath and straightened his

shoulders but said nothing. Having friends in high places wasn't such a bad thing after all.

"Here," she said, holding a silver flask out to me after we'd entered our dorm room and shut the door behind us. "It'll calm you down," she explained when I didn't take it right away. "Take some of the edge off, if you know what I mean."

I took a long swallow and choked. The strong, acrid flavor of the liquor burned down my throat. Confused, I looked up at her from where I sat on the bed. "You really aren't who I thought you were, you know."

She rolled her light brown eyes, pulling her albino rabbit onto her lap as she sat down on the edge of her own bed across from me.

She absently began stroking its soft fur. "Don't get me wrong," she said. "My uncle is great. He's a good man…" she trailed off and I wondered if she was trying to convince me or herself.

"But he has these—these *expectations* of me. As the headmaster of the academy, but also as a council member, he expects me to be…" She pursed her lips, considering how best to explain it.

"Someone other than yourself," I offered. It didn't make me feel better to learn the man responsible for ensuring I served my punishment was *also* a member of the Arcane Council. But it wasn't surprising. Of course, he would be.

She nodded. "Exactly. And I get it, really, I do. He's kind of a big deal, and what I do affects his image. It sucks, but that's the way it is… and I don't have anyone else."

I knew what that was like. Trying so hard to fit into a mold created for you. Granted, other than never being able to set down roots or make friends, I never really minded living the life of a traveling gypsy. And Leo and Lara mostly let me do as I pleased.

But since coming to the academy, I felt the pressure to conform. It was suffocating. And I didn't even come from a rich family with expectations. Not for the first time, I felt as though I could trust Bianca, regardless of her connection with the headmaster.

I gritted my teeth and stood, pushing the flask back into Bianca's hand. She took a small sip before twisting the cap back on and tucking it away into a drawer in her vanity.

"They're my familiars," I said before I could stop myself.

Her face scrunched up in confusion and she leaned back, her eyes searching my face. I saw the moment what I'd said clicked in her mind. Her mouth fell slack and her eyes widened. "No freaking way!" she exclaimed, sitting bolt upright. "That's —" she started, managing to look shocked, confused, excited, and horrified all at once. "But that's impossible."

I fell back on my bed, staring up at the yellowed stucco ceiling. "Apparently not."

"Shit," she said, and I heard the springs of her mattress creak as she stood, and the sound of her feet as she paced back and forth between our beds. "If you're serious, we have to tell somebody. This is, like, the biggest thing to happen in the witching community since—"

"No!" I interrupted her, pushing myself up onto my elbows. "No, Bianca, you have to promise me you won't tell anyone. Please."

She stopped pacing. "Why?"

"Because if our—*my* plan works," I said, hurriedly correcting my use of *our*. I wasn't yet ready to tell anyone about Elias Fitzgerald's offer to help me, or the strange connection we seemed to share. She wouldn't understand… I wasn't even sure I did. "There will be nothing to tell."

"I don't understand. What do you mean there won't be anything to tell?"

I licked my suddenly dry lips and clasped my hands together, squeezing tight. "Because—I'm going to sever the bond."

Bianca was appalled at my plan to sever the

familiar bond. I could tell she was still reeling from learning that something like bonding to an Enduran —never mind *two* Endurans—was even possible, but it was finding out my intent to break the bond that seemed to shock her the most.

She'd looked at her own familiar, with a sad fondness in her gaze, likely imagining what it would be like not to have her.

I couldn't say I fully understood that feeling. But even though the bond between Cal, Adrian, and I was still new and hadn't had a chance to fully strengthen, the thought of cutting them away made my pulse quicken and my stomach turn.

It was unnatural to break a familiar's bond. And the wrongness of the idea made my skin crawl. But I'd promised them I'd find a way, and I intended to.

Which was how I found myself searching the academy for Elias after dinner. I hoped he'd been able find something, or at least had a lead or two. I would have to tell him about what happened in the woods, and of our new time constraints. We now had seven days to make the impossible possible.

After what felt like at least an hour of wandering the hallways, I found him where I'd first bumped into him. He had his nose in an old tome, furiously scouring the pages with brows knit together and a tight jaw as he came around the corner from the faculty wing of the building.

I wondered if he had an office down there.

As though sensing my presence, he looked up, doing a double take when he realized it was me coming toward him. Was that a small smile twitching at the corner of his mouth? I grinned at him, rushing past Headmaster Sterling's office on my toes. Trying to make as little noise as possible.

"What are you doing down here?" he asked, looking up the hallway the way I'd come, and back toward the fork that led to the faculty offices and living quarters. All was quiet.

His adams apple bobbed.

"Looking for you," I replied, remembering why I had to come find him, and frowning. "I have to talk to you," I said, more seriously, my voice breathy with anxiety. He tucked his book under his arm, and reached out a hand to reassure me, setting it lightly on my the spot just above my elbow. His palm was warm against my perpetually cool skin, and I quivered at the contact.

He recoiled as though shocked, snapping me from the momentary euphoria.

"What is it?" he asked, his tone clipped and voice low. "Is everything alright?" Elias tucked his hand—the one he'd touched me with—into the pocket of his jacket, glancing at it as though it was a wild animal that needed leashing. He wore a beat-up leather coat with what looked like woolen lining. It suited him.

He must've been on his way out to his cabin for the night. I was certain he'd never dress in leather and jeans in front of the students or other faculty. They seemed, I don't know… too *poise* for that.

After a deep and calming breath, I relayed to him everything that'd happened in the woods as quickly as I could—omitting only the part about telling Bianca. I watched as his expression became more strained, his eyes more dark with each word I spoke.

"You did what?" he nearly shouted when I'd finished, and suddenly I felt very small.

"I had to see what they wanted," I snapped, the words coming out laced with indignation and something more like venom. "What would you have had me do?"

"Not put yourself in danger," he spat back, his eyes stormier than usual, shrouded in darkness.

Just then a door clicked open and the headmaster's voice floated down the hallway toward us. I jumped, letting loose a short gasp before Elias grabbed me by the hand and whirled my body into a small alcove a few feet from where we'd been standing.

He pressed his own body flush against mine so we both could fit. His fingers drew the simple warding sigil behind us, it lit up and glowed blue before it faded into a rippling shield at his back.

There were two voices coming closer to the hall-way. Two deep, aged baritones, one I recognized to be Atticus Sterling. But I wasn't focusing on *them.*

Elias stood very still, and with my back against the wall, I had nowhere to move. My hands rested against his chest, and I could feel the strong, insistent thrumming of his heartbeat beneath the wiry muscle. His cold mountain pine and spice scent clouded my mind and before I realized what I was doing, I had rested my cheek against him.

I couldn't help but notice how his hand still grasped my waist, keeping me pressed against the wall. I arched my back and lifted my chin to look up at him. I found him staring down at me, his nostrils flared slightly, his eyes hungry and intense. His lips parted and something did a little summersault deep in my belly.

And then he froze.

He cocked his head, tilting one ear closer to the ward to hear.

Oh, no! Were they coming this way?

I struggled to hear them, too, forcing the drumming of my pulse to calm with shallow, quiet breaths. Compelling the tension to ease from my limbs.

"...I can assure you the girl knows nothing, and

all the other loose ends were taken care of long ago." Who was the headmaster talking to? I listened harder.

"Mmmm," said the other man. "And this *professor* of yours—the woman who was asking questions?"

Elias and I shared a look, his grip on my waist tightened infinitesimally. They were talking about Ms. Granger. They had to be. She was the only female professor at the academy. But what had she been asking questions about? And why was that so bad?

I got the distinct feeling that this was *not* a conversation meant to be overheard.

"A former friend of Alistair's, but no more than that." My hand flew up to cover my mouth, and my breathing hitched at the mention of his name. Could they have been talking about my father? What were the chances that I'd only just learned of him the day before—from Ms. Granger no less— and now the headmaster was speaking to this other man about someone with same name. It seemed too big a coincidence.

Elias narrowed his eyes at me, mouthed, *you okay?*

I didn't respond. Just held up a finger to hush him. I needed to be able to hear.

"She is no threat," Headmaster Sterling assured the other man. "I'm sure of it."

"See it stays that way," said the other man in an offhanded, bored sort of tone.

"Yes, Magistrate. I shall."

No. Freaking. Way.

The Magistrate was here. Freaking *Godric Montgomery*—the *head* of the Arcane Council and the guy who oversaw the entire witching community in the USA was at Arcane Arts Academy, talking to the headmaster about... about my dad?

Elias was shocked, too, and searched the airspace above my head for an answer. His expression was thoughtful as he tried to make sense of it. When he met my gaze, his expression softened, and he brought up his hand to rest against my cheek. I sighed at the comfort the small contact brought. "What is it, Harper?" he whispered when Godric's retreating footsteps grew further away, and the door to Sterling's office clicked back shut.

I looked away, unable to hold Elias' gaze. "They were talking about my father."

11

———

y tea had grown cold. I was too
frazzled to drink it, or to do
anything more than sit stupefied on the tiny loveseat
in Elias' cabin. When the hallways were clear again,
Elias had wrapped a ward around us like a cloak
and we'd snuck out to his cabin.

I was impressed—not just anyone could hold up
a ward while in motion, and not for as long as it
took for us to cross the academy grounds and get
under cover of the trees. But he'd done it without
breaking a sweat.

That didn't matter, though. And I hardly
noticed how effortless his power came—the riot of
thoughts crashing and running in my mind made
any other mundane thought evaporate. I couldn't

make sense of it. They *had* to be talking about my dad. But why?

"Your father was a powerful witch," Elias said from where he sat in one of the wrought-iron chairs opposite me. I'd told him who my father was, and he'd known the name right away. I supposed dear old dad had made something of a name for himself before he died.

"What do you think they meant?" I asked him, setting down the cold tea-cup on a small pedestal table beside the arm of the loveseat. "And why the hell was Godric Montgomerey here?"

He blew out a breath and scratched at the short hairs at the back of his neck. The glow of the simpering fire in the hearth to our left cast an orange glow over his cheek. "Your guess is as good as mine. I've never seen him here before, but Sterling being on the council... well it may not be uncommon." He shrugged.

I squirmed against the soft cushion beneath me, leaning in to rest my elbows against my knees and rub my eyes. A dull ache had formed behind them, alluding to the migraine to come. I was prone to them when I was younger, but I hadn't had one in years. They were so strong that not even magic could soothe the pain.

When I looked up again, Elias was studying me, and he quickly looked away.

"Why do you do that?" I asked and watched his temple twitch with the flexing of his jaw.

He steeled himself before he turned back to me. "Do what?" he asked, palms up as though he was genuinely confused. Not for the first time, I wondered if I was wrong about the connection I felt between us. A fiery blush sparked up the back of my neck. I shook it off.

"Nothing," I replied, biting the inside of my cheek to check my emotions. "Can you," I started, pausing, unsure whether to ask even more of him— but I *had* to know. And connection or not, I somehow knew I could trust the man before me. "I mean, could you possibly find out exactly what happened to my dad? I've never known how he died," I laughed nervously. "I've never known anything about him actually... I only just learned my last name yesterday."

Elias nodded to himself, considering my request with pursed lips and hands clenched tightly together. He cracked his knuckles. "I can tell how much it's bothering you... and if it matters that much, then I will do my best to find out," he said, and I sat up straighter, smiling—some of my vigor renewed. "But," he added, and I deflated. "I believe we have more pressing matters to attend to—like breaking your witch familiar bond with those two Endurans."

Right.

"Have you found anything?" I asked him, noticing how much more filled the small bistro table was with documents and tomes, and how they'd spread like a disease to cover the top of his nightstand and the kitchen countertop. Some were even piled beside his bed, where I saw Fallon, his familiar napping in the shadows.

"No," he breathed. "And honestly, I'm starting to think such a spell doesn't exist." My blood curdled in my veins. I had only six more days until I became dog chow, and we had *nothing*. "The only solution I can think of is to *create* a new spell."

But that was crazy. There was a reason new spells hadn't been created since the Codex was written hundreds of years before. It was dangerous and yielded unpredictable results. The sigils and incantations created almost always ended catastrophically—or more commonly, did absolutely nothing.

"That's insane," I told him, sitting back and throwing my hands up, exasperated. My head throbbed even more than it had been a moment before.

"It is."

I pinched the bridge of my nose.

The cushions rebounded as he sidled up next to me. I dared a peek at him, gritting my teeth against the urge to reach out and run my fingertips along the stubble on his jaw. Elias pulled my hand away from my face, holding it lightly as though it were made of porcelain. He set it down in my lap and sighed. "It may be the only way."

THAT NIGHT I tossed and turned in my sleep. Falling in and out of consciousness. The migraine so painful it felt like my skull would split in two. No longer a dull ache behind my eye sockets, the stabbing, throbbing sensation radiated from my forehead over the precipice of my skull and down the back of my head.

I cried out, but I couldn't be certain if I was awake or dreaming. Snippets of hallucinatory visions and nightmares danced against my eyelids, interspersed with periods of deep, fathomless blackness that had me questioning my sanity.

I thought I heard Bianca murmuring an incantation sometime in the night. And at one point a searing yellow glow assaulted my eyes. I didn't know if it was real, or if it was a vivid nightmare my mind created from the pain. And later, the high-pitched whine of animal cries outside echoed down my ear canals, making my blood run cold.

Or maybe that was the fever...

I shook with an intense chill, unable to get warm

no matter how tightly I wrapped the blanket around my frail bones.

My magic roiled within me, stinging at the inside of my flesh and making me spasm and contract with the effort of holding it in. My bed shook beneath me. The migraine stabbed at my brain with each jolted movement. I cried out and a reverberating groan of thunder shook the window pane in the room.... or maybe it had been a growl...

My throat was so dry, and my heart skipped several beats before it came back with a fury—pounding forcefully as though my blood had thickened and it needed to work twice as hard to pump it through. My eyes flew open at the strength of it, and in a lucid moment I realized I was floating... and *moving*...

I caught a glimpse of wavy brown hair with streaks of gold and bronze and worried deep brown eyes. It was Ms. Granger.

"Will she be alright?" I heard Bianca's shrill voice call out to Granger as the professor levitated me quickly down the hallway behind her.

I moaned, clutching at my head—trying to keep it from bursting. I cried out when a lance of pain shot through it from one end to the other, and the hair-raising crackle and *crash* of lightning resounded all around me. The electricity in the atmosphere sparked in my veins.

"The new girl's finally lost it," I heard Kendra say—her voice trailing behind me through the hallways along with the snicker of her loyal band of followers. I gritted my teeth, and the lighting came down again, hitting some part of the academy with a *boom* loud and powerful enough to wake the dead.

The lights flickered, and the girls in the hallways squealed and screamed.

"Clear the hallways—get back to bed!" Granger shouted and I heard her heeled shoes walking a little faster.

"It's alright," she said more calmly, and I felt the brush of cool fingertips against my sweat-slicked temple. "It'll be alright."

I sealed my eyes back closed against the onslaught of light flashing through the windows from the storm, and my breath caught at the sound of two wolves howling. The sound haunting and beautiful. The twin howls came together to form a tormented harmony that wrapped itself like a vise around my heart.

And then my pulse slowed...

Slowed....

Then there was only darkness and blissful silence.

12

When I awoke Saturday morning, peeling my eyelids back slowly in preparation for the pain, I was pleasantly surprised to find there wasn't any. I blinked into the bright lights in the wide room. Getting my bearings.

Bianca was asleep in a chair at the end of the bed where I was laying. I was covered in a thin white sheet and still dressed in my smelly night clothes. A grinding sound pulled my attention and I found Ms. Granger standing at a countertop to my right, grinding herbs with a mortar and pestle.

From the array of jars and bottles, and the bunches of dried herbs hanging from the ceiling, I would have to assume this was the academy's infirmary.

And then I remembered.

The storm and the lightning. The other girls in the dormitory watching as Ms. Granger carried me out through the hallways as I writhed in pain and moaned and shouted. *Crap.*

Kendra's voice came back the clearest... *the new girl's finally lost it...*

She might not have been wrong... for a while, I thought I had.

"Oh, good," Granger said, turning at the sound of my whining groan. "You're awake. How do you feel?"

"Better," I replied, pushing the hair away from my face. My hands came away oily. My hair feeling like it'd been drenched it in hot soup and then left to dry. "Ugh," I groaned again. I needed a shower. *Bad.*

Ms. Granger tipped the fine powder from the mortar into a small bowl of steaming water, swirling the contents. The scents of lavender and frankincense wafted over to me, along with something bitter and tangy that made me want to plug my nose.

"Here," she said. "Drink this. It will help renew your strength," she said in a whisper-soft voice, glancing at Bianca where she slept with her head tilted back against the high backed chair, mouth agape, and one eye half-open to expose the whites.

I took the bowl, clasping it between my palms.

The warmth seeped into my skin, and I sighed at the release of tension.

Now that she'd said it, I found I did feel weakened. My bones felt heavy, and my mind was already tired to the point of wanting a nap even though I'd only just woken up. But it was always like this with my migraines. *I thought this shit was over,* I thought to myself, putting the bowl to my lips to take a small sip.

Granger sat on the edge of the narrow bed, leveling a motherly stare at me. "Are these... migraines of yours chronic? Do they happen often?"

I took another swallow of the warm potion mixture, making a face at the bitter aftertaste. "No," I began, but then amended. "Well, they aren't anymore. I used to get them all the time, but they stopped a few years ago."

"When you came into your powers?"

My brows furrowed, and I thought back to the last time I'd had a migraine like that. She was right, it'd been only days before I first came into my powers.

"Yeah."

She offered me a warm smile and told me not to worry, taking the now empty bowl from my hands and rising to place it back on the counter.

"I've got to go check on something," she said,

turning back to me for a moment, before making for the hall, pausing in the doorway to give me a look that managed to be reassuring at the same time as it was puzzled. "Try to rest. The revival potion should take effect

quickly."

I nodded, and she was gone.

"You look better," Bianca said and I nearly jumped out of my skin, my hand flying to my chest to contain the wild *pitter patter* of my pulse. "Whoa, didn't mean to scare you," she said, holding her hands up in an I'm-not-gonna-eat-you gesture.

"Aren't you supposed to be visiting with your brothers?" I asked her after I'd caught my breath, trying to stretch out a kink in my neck.

Bianca waved off the question with an eye-roll and a tiny smirk. "They can wait a bit. They'll understand when I tell them my roomie had a catatonic fit and nearly blew up the academy."

"What—"

"Oh," she said, her brows rising as she leant in. "*And* your—um—*familiars* were outside our

window last night, howling and whining like mad. It was super annoying."

So, I hadn't been dreaming that. But... "Wait, back up. I didn't start that storm. People can't honestly think *I* caused that."

Bianca clucked her tongue and gave a slow,

exaggerated shrug. "All I know is that the moment you passed out, the storm stopped. The thunder, the lightning, the rain—all of it. Like it was never even there."

It had to be a coincidence. There were only a handful of witches in recorded history who could affect the weather, and those bloodlines were long dead. Even Bianca didn't look like she fully believed it, and she was the one telling me it'd happened.

I gulped past a large lump in my throat, ready to refute what she'd said when a figure appeared in the doorway and stole the words from my mouth.

"So, what's all this fuss about?" Headmaster Sterling asked in his deep baritone, looking from Bianca to me and back again. His deep gray suit brought out the silver running through the black in his beard and hair, and the fluorescent lights made his dark eyes gleam as they

pierced through me, impatiently waiting for a response.

"Just a migraine," I said simply.

"Is that all?" he replied with a fabricated smile, his tone far from relieved and more toward conde-scending.

"I'm—" I began, but he turned to his niece, who was smiling up at him guiltily, as though she were caught playing with something she shouldn't have.

"Bianca," he said. "Shouldn't you be on your way? I know your brothers are eager to see you."

It was the nicest sounding dismissal I'd ever heard.

Bianca gave me a sheepish grin before rising from her chair. "Yes, uncle. You're right. Now that I've seen Harper is alright, I'll go to them. May I portal myself?"

No, I wanted to say, *don't leave me with him!*

"Mmm," he said with a nod, and Bianca scurried from the room, calling back to me over her shoulder. "I'll see you tomorrow, Harper."

Headmaster Sterling knotted his weathered hands behind his back, and lifted his chin to take a long breath, his gaze never leaving me. I cowered under the pressure of his stare. *Why wasn't he saying anything?* After another beat of silence, he spoke, his voice booming after the momentary silence. "You gave my students and faculty quite a scare."

"I didn't mean—"

"I hope these *disturbances* are not a regular occurrence," he said, grimacing. "If they are, I may be forced to petition the council to have you placed somewhere they are better equipped to deal with those sorts of *ailments.*"

The thought of leaving Elias and Bianca... and

even my familiars left a sour taste in my mouth and a pit in my stomach.

Sterling really was the *worst* sort of asshole. It was just a *migraine.* It wasn't as though I'd done anything on purpose.

What a dick.

"No, of course not. I—"

"Good," he said, cutting me off gain. "Glad to hear it."

Granger returned to the room, scowling at the back of Sterling's head. I wondered if she'd heard what he said.

"Ah, Granger," he said by way of greeting.

She set a breakfast tray down on my bed and my stomach growled audibly. It was filled with fruits, nuts and buttery toast... and *coffee?* I hadn't smelled the beautiful aroma of coffee in

over a week. My mouth watered at the sight of it. All they had laid out for the students was herbal tea in the mornings. I wondered who's terrible idea it was to leave coffee out of the morning line-up. We were teenagers, not children.

I snagged it from the tray, chugging it down with barely a care that it was scalding my tongue. And she'd even put two sugars in! As if she'd known exactly how I liked it.

"I can take it from here," she said brazenly to

the headmaster with a close-lipped smile. "I'm sure you have more pressing matters to attend to."

"Hmmm. That I do." He cast me one last side-long glance before leaving without another word."

Is he always like that?" I asked when I was certain he was out of hearing range.

"What? You mean a total ass?" she asked, one thin brow raised and a smirk playing at the corner of mouth.

Shocked, and pleasantly surprised someone else agreed with me, I burst out laughing. "Yeah. That."

Ms. Granger chuckled, trying to keep her lips tightly closed to reign herself in. "Pretty much all the time, yes."

I shook my head, relieved.

Granger popped a grape from my tray into her mouth, one hand on her hip. "Seriously, though, he's always had a problem with women in power," she mused, turning to face me once more. "And you, my dear, are *very* powerful."

She couldn't possibly think the storm was because of me, too… could she? And then a more dangerous thought crossed my mind—what if it *was* me?

"I haven't seen an equal to your power in all the years I've taught here—in all my life, really… except maybe Alistair, but even he couldn't draw lightning down from the sky."

I didn't want to think about what'd happened the night before anymore. It was scary and embarrassing, and I didn't want to believe it was true. Sure, being powerful was great and all, who wouldn't want to be a strong witch? But being *that* powerful was dangerous. I could hurt someone—or a lot of someone's, especially with my inherent clumsiness…

It was impossible for witches like that to fly under the radar. I didn't want to be noticed, or fought over, or asked to do things I didn't want to do. I wanted to be left the hell alone.

But she reminded me of something. "Hey, did you ask Headmaster Sterling about my dad?"

"Yes," she said, looking at me quizzically. "I inquired because Alistair—I mean, *your father* had been quite a wealthy man. I wanted to know if anything remained to be transferred to you."

"Oh." He had been wealthy?

"And," she continued, looking away with a slight roll of her eyes. "I had also requested to review any files Sterling might have access to in the academy's files, or in the Arcane Council's. I wanted to be able to give you more information about him—about what happened to him," she said, huffing. "But my request was denied."

I sat up a little straighter, unable to stop the shiver from rolling up my back. "Why?"

She gave a one-shoulder shrug. "Something about *confidentiality*," she said. "*But*, he did agree to look into your father's holdings. You would need to submit to an origin test, of course, to be able to lay claim to Alistair's properties and financial holdings."

I was dumbfounded. Had she said *properties*? As in, plural? All this time I could've been rich. I imagined a younger version of myself, growing up in a grand mansion, never having to want for anything. I wanted to want it. Who wouldn't want to be rich and have nice things? But… I didn't. If I'd grown up like that, who was to say I wouldn't have turned out like Kendra, or one of her minions?

I felt guilty just thinking it. Remembering Leo laughing as he pulled me along the ice-rink, telling me to *push and glide*, not *stomp and scream*. And Lara, gathering my hair into a smooth braid so it wouldn't tangle while I slept.

"Ms. Granger, can I ask you a favor?"

"Diana," she corrected, and I beamed. "Of course. Ask away."

13

---

*D*iana was more than happy to show me the sigil and it's accompanying incantation to send messages to someone outside the academy. She seemed surprised I didn't already know it. But I'd never had anyone I needed to communicate *with* before. Leo and Lara were either always with me, or they weren't far.

She'd offered to show me where the communication booth was at the academy. It being the only place where the wards wouldn't block the transference of messages. It was where all the other students went to 'call' their parents and friends. I'd lied and said I already knew where it was.

No one could know who I was calling. I was supposed to be an orphan with no guardians. I was sure Sterling wouldn't hesitate to throw them into

Kalzir if it meant being rid of me. Which was why I was rushing through the vacant hallways on my way out to the woods. I'd have to get outside the wards, and I didn't know how far they stretched. I hadn't paid enough attention to remember where exactly I'd felt it before.

Looking back to make sure no one followed or was watching from the windows overlooking the backyard, I ducked into the trees and sped deeper into the foliage. The ward extended further than I thought it would, but after only a few moments, I felt the telltale bristling of my skin as I passed through. It wavered and shimmered as it spat me out on the other side, quickly going back to being completely invisible.

Here goes nothing, I thought, rubbing my palms together.

The only private place I'd be able to reach them would be in the caravan, so, I hoped they just happened to be in it on a sunny Saturday afternoon.

Remembering Diana's instructions, I began to draw on the power I would need to do the spell. Letting it climb my veins as though they were vines—to bloom and expand. I tipped my head back at the rush of power as it settled in my core. There was nothing better than the feeling right before doing a spell, when your body was the most full of magical energy. It was tantalizing, like a lover's touch. Beckoning. Coaxing you to your release.

I'd have to be quick, I reminded myself. If I was caught performing magic unsupervised off of academy grounds...*again*... I wasn't sure what would happen. But I knew it wouldn't be good.

I drew the sigil Diana had drawn in ink on my palm into the air in front of me. The tip of my finger leaving a bright, shimmering blue trail as it moved. And then, I drew a large circle around it, and whispered the incantation like she taught me. "Ostium revelare."

Visualizing the inside of the caravan, I closed my eyes and tapped twice on the sigil as though knocking at a doorway. When I opened my eyes again the symbol was gone, and inside the glowing ring materialized an image of the inside of the caravan. It worked!

The top bunk where I used to sleep was still covered with my dark blue hand-knit blanket, a gift Lara had made me when I turned thirteen. But unlike usual, the bed was made, and boxes and bins of jewelry and potions were weighing down the old mattress.

Leo's french press sat in the sink with two dirty mugs instead of three.

The image moved slightly, and I realized I could see the road through the windshield as they took a turn. I grinned, holding back a shriek, almost bouncing on my feet. The radio was on low, but neither of them were singing like they usually did. I could just see the edges of their faces from where the communication mirror had opened up near the back of the caravan.

"Leo?" I said gently, not wanting to spook them and cause an accident. "Lara?"

Lara whipped around her seat, her small blue eyes bugging out of her tiny head. "Harper?" she exclaimed, fighting with the button to unlatch her seatbelt. Leo slammed on the breaks, and yanked the wheel to the right to pull the caravan onto the side of highway, the breaks screeching in protest as he ground the old metal beast to a jarring standstill.

Lara finally got her seatbelt off, and they tripped over each other in their haste to get to the mirror. "Oh, honey!" Lara said, her hands clenched into little fists near her face. I could tell she hated that she couldn't reach out and hug me. I hated it, too. But that wasn't how this spell worked. It wasn't a portal, but more like… magical FaceTime.

"How are you? Is everything alright?" Lara blurted.

"We've been worried sick," Leo added, his gaze roving over my face and shoulders, making sure I was alright. Leo wasn't the buff type, but I had no doubts that if anyone were to try to harm me, he'd protect me the best he could. With his small frame and crafters hands, he was more a lover than a fighter. They both were.

My eyes pricked, and I reigned in the urge to cry at the sight of them. "I'm alright," I told them, maintaining the smile when it tried to falter with the lie. I tipped my head toward the woods behind me. "I suppose you already know where I am?"

Lara nodded quickly, her thin white-gold hair falling over her teary eyes. "How is it?" she asked in a hopeful voice. "We were so relieved when we found out where they'd sent you. When Gato transferred your message to Leo to not to come after you… well, we didn't know what to think."

"We had to use both our powers combined and an amplification spell to find you. They must have strong wards around the whole place." Leo said, and I could hear the awe in his voice. He'd always wanted to be able to send me to a place like AAA, and often talked about finding ways to make extra money so he could do it—even though we both knew it was an outlandish thought.

I nodded. "They do."

"Good thing we had some of your hair or we never would've been able to find you." Lara added in a rush.

"I knew you would." I tucked my hair back and readjusted my headband. "And—*um*, the academy's great," I told them, and found truth in the words. The place really was starting to grow on me, or at least, some of the people in it were.

And now, looking into the hopeful eyes of my makeshift family, I realized it would be foolish—not to mention *idiotic* to not take this opportunity to learn and strengthen my magic. A thousand other less fortunate witches would kill to be in my shoes. Little did they know all they had to do was get arrested and have some old council coot take pity on them and wave the tuition fee.

As though sensing what I was thinking, Leo's and Lara's expressions changed in synchronicity like only they could do. "We aren't upset about what happened. We wanted you to know that." Lara said.

"No one was hurt, and we know your magic is… *difficult* to control. It was our fault for leaving you alone."

I sighed, unable to meet their gazes. "No. It wasn't you fau—"

"Yes, it was," Lara interrupted me in that gentle way she often did. "And we are the ones who should have been punished."

"Your quick thinking saved us from—" Leo dragged in a tight breath and rubbed at the bit of scruff on his narrow jaw. "Well, if it weren't for your…" I could tell he was having trouble saying it. He was always crap at saying thank you.

I smiled at him. "You're welcome," I said to them both with a little laugh. "I mean, it's not like I was sent to Kalzir or burned at the stake. Pretty sure I'm the one who got the better end of the stick. Who's going to label your potions, now?" I joked.

They both laughed, grinning. The relief plain on both their faces.

The edges of the mirror began to fade, and the glowing ring around it was waning. Time was running out.

"Anyways, don't worry about me. I'll call as much as I can, but if I get caught using magic off the grounds—"

"Don't worry yourself. We don't want you getting in any trouble," Leo said, sounding gruff, his throat thick with tears he'd never admit to having. "Just study hard, and get good grades, and… and…"

"I'll see you before you know it," I finished for him. It was our trademark phrase anytime one of us had to leave for more than a day. The words came out strained, and I clenched my jaw.

"See you before you know it," they both replied, and I swiped a hand through the glowing ring— dissolving the image a second before the sob broke free from my chest.

I hadn't realized how much I'd missed them. But seeing them made it so much more real. I wouldn't see them again until I graduated in *four years* —barring some sort of miracle. I clutched my chest and allowed myself to sink down to my knees against the mossy ground.

I cursed the tears that fell. What *was* this shit? I didn't cry. I couldn't even remember the last time I had. It might've been years. It didn't matter what life threw at me, I always took it in stride. Finding the silver-lining or making one myself. *This isn't so bad*, I convinced myself. *This is not the end of the damned world.*

And the tears began to dry, and my breathing evened out. *There you go. That's it. Just breathe.*

I didn't know how long I'd been there, but the sun had already begun walking along it's well-worn path back down toward the horizon, lighting the sky pink and violet in its wake. And I remembered something Lara always used to say when I'd had a bad day. *The sun will rise on a new day whether you're ready to face it or not, my girl. Best to show it some teeth.*

They were an odd sort, my guardians. But I wouldn't change them for the world. I wouldn't change anything about the way I was brought up. How much of this country I'd gotten to see. I smirked. Maybe... maybe *I* was the lucky one—not these spoiled academy kids.

With my resolve strengthened, and the phantom

voice of Lara in my head, I felt ready to return to the academy and whatever waited for me there.

The muffled sound of footsteps against dirt had my hackles rising. I spun at the crunch of a twig to my right.

But it was only Fallon, his ears laid flat against his head as he neared me. I didn't reach out to him, afraid to scare him off. The silver fox sniffed at my hands and looked up at me with curious dark reddish-brown eyes. He was beautiful. A few seconds later Elias stepped into the small copse of trees, and Fallon skittered back over to stand behind him.

Elias held a branch away from his face as he stepped through, looking only mildly surprised to find me alone in the woods for the second time that week.

"I thought I might find you out here," he said lightly, stuffing one hand into the pocket of his leather jacket and extending the other to help me stand. "I heard what happened last night. Are you alright?"

The ball reformed in my chest, expanding painfully. I winced and looked away from his worried blue eyes. "I don't know," I whispered.

He rubbed the backs of my knuckles with his thumb. His hands far warmer than mine. It was soothing and electrifying all at once. I wanted to melt into his touch—for him to take all the bad things away—make me forget, if only for a little while.

"I'm sorry all of this is happening to you. It must be a lot to deal with." He reached out with his other hand and wiped what remained of the tears from my cheeks, sighing. "You are so strong, Harper. And brave."

Was I? I didn't feel strong... and certainly not brave. I felt small and weak. Frail.

When I gathered enough confidence, I lifted my chin to look him in the eyes, catching him as his gaze fell quickly to my lips before darting away.

He couldn't have been more than twenty-five, maybe twenty-six. The youngest teacher at the academy by far. If we were just two people, not a teacher and his student, would he finally give in to his desires? Would I?

I'd only ever been kissed a handful of times, and they were sloppy, inexperienced boys. What would it be like to be kissed by a *man?* I didn't know, but I sure as hell wanted to find out.

As though sensing my thoughts, Elias' lips parted as he moved in closer, dipping his head low so his dark hair fell forward to shadow his eyes. But the inner turmoil he faced was still visible, gleaming behind his storm-cloud iris'.

"What the *hell* was that last night?"

Elias and I jumped apart, and he shoved me behind him, assuming a fighting stance at my front, his hand raised—the glow of his activated power swirled around his fingers. "Fallon, home," he commanded his familiar, and the fox hissed at the Endurans before he sped back through the trees. His bushy silver-dipped tail bobbing behind him.

"Who the hell is this clown?" Cal said, coming out from behind Adrian, his eyes glowing faintly with his urge to shift.

I pushed Elias out of the way, stepping forward to face them. "It's alright. It's them," I told Elias. "My familiars."

"Ugh," Cal said with a twisted scowl. "Don't call us that."

Elias didn't back down but didn't stop me either. He remained at my side, and I could feel his magic electrifying the air around us both.

Cal and Adrian looked me over, something like relief flashing in their eyes. I felt it, too. The internal release. The bond strengthening me—and them.

"What are you doing here?"

"We sensed you were outside the wards, and we had to talk," Adrian explained, and a blush crawled up my neck when I noticed just how *low* his cut-off jean shorts rode on his hips. Showing the dips leading down to... I shook my head. The bond between me and my familiars was a hard thing to ignore. Why couldn't they have been ugly? Or, you know, *not* incredibly sexy wolf shifters. I'd have taken literally *anything* else.

"Last night—what was that? You were... in so much *pain*. We could feel it."

I bit the inside of my cheek, not wanting to get into it. What did they care, anyway? "Nothing. Just a bad migraine," I said, wanting so badly for it to be the truth. Knowing it probably wasn't. Before either of them could answer, I added. "This is Elias." I cleared my throat as I snapped myself out of it, gesturing to him.

"He—um—he's helping me find a way to break the bond."

Elias nodded. "I'm sorry this happened to you. I can't say I know how you both must feel, but I can assure you this was not Harper's fault." He reached out and grabbed my hand. My heart did a little flip. "And we're doing everything we can—"

There it was again. That *we* word.

"It doesn't matter who's fault it is," Cal snapped, regarding Elias with... with jealousy? No, that wasn't right. What reason would he have to be jealous? Maybe it was a wolf thing. Territorial or whatever.

"Look," Cal said, cutting in front of Adrian. "We can't take this much longer, and Atlas knows something's up. It won't be long before he figures it out or commands it out of us."

"We had a deal," I began. "A week—"

Adrian's nostrils flared, and I could sense his temper wouldn't be reigned in much longer. "The deal won't matter if we receive a direct command from our alpha. We have to bend to his will—like it or not." And I could tell, Adrian did *not* like it.

"If he thinks the only way to sever the bond is to... to kill you, then that will be his command."

"What do you care," I croaked, thinking about how it would feel if my own familiars tried to kill me because their *alpha* told them too. "You want this bond broken. What does is matter to you how it gets broken?"

I stepped forward, jabbing a finger into Adrian's solid, tan chest. "You don't scare me," I said, not allowing so much as a trace of the deep seeded fear I truly felt to taint my voice. He growled, and his eyes glowed vibrant gold in the growing dark.

Cal's hands curled into claws, his sharp nails pushing out from his nail beds.

"Harper," I heard Elias warn, but he didn't make a move to intervene. Not yet.

I ignored him.

My haughty stare was unwavering as I held Adrian's furious gaze. "I'm not going to be afraid of you. I *won't* be afraid of my own damned familiars!"

"You should be," Adrian replied in a voice so deep and so calm, it made my insides tremble.

I staggered back, the momentary burst of angered confidence fading fast. The magic laced adrenaline coursing through my veins wore off, and my shoulders slumped. I stepped back.

The space between us was filled with unasked and unanswered questions. Tense. The silence roaring in my ears.

It was Elias who broke it. "We haven't found anything yet," he said, and I saw Cal's face fall and a muscle twitch in Adrian's jaw. "But we'll keep trying. What you're asking—you have to understand, it's never been done before."

Cal nodded to Elias. "We'll do our best to honor the week we agreed upon. But we can make no promises." Then he turned his attention to me, and I saw a longing in his stare, but more than that—I felt it. A thick vein protruded in his neck, and his claws lengthened. He was trying to fight the call of the bond.

Adrian was, too. And I was weakened by their efforts to keep me at a distance. The harder they pushed, the more feeble I felt, and the more sluggish my magic. Fighting it wasn't doing them any favors either. It was driving them to the point of madness.

If they accepted it, it wouldn't be so hard... or so draining, for all of us.

"Have—have you thought about letting the bond take hold?" I asked them, directing the question more toward Cal, since he seemed more receptive to it. I felt Elias stiffen beside me.

"We will never surrender to a witch's will." It was Adrian who answered.

They didn't understand. I hurried to explain. "No, I mean—just for now. It would be easier."

Adrian scoffed and Cal looked away, his lips pursed.

"And the bond isn't one-sided," I added, stepping forward again, imploring them to understand. "The bond goes both ways. You would submit to me, yes. But I would also submit to you. It's a… a partnership. Not a master and servant kind of thing."

"She's right," Elias said, and Cal shot him a cutting glare, looking doubtful, crossing his arms over his chest.

"We see it differently," Cal said.

Adrian threw his hands up in the air, and shouted. "Enough of this. We're done talking. We'll be back in a few days, and you'd better hope you've got good news."

"Is that a threat?" Elias bellowed, his body going rigid beneath his leather jacket, reassuming his protective stance in front of me.

Adrian shook his head. "No. It's fair warning."

14

They were gone within seconds, first walking back the way they'd come through the darkened forest, and then the sound of a howl broke the eerie quiet, and we knew they'd shifted and would be miles away in only a few moments. Shifters were *fast*.

"Come on, we should go before it gets too dark," Elias said, holding out his arm for me. I took it gratefully, knowing that in the blinding blarc of the sun just before twilight, I'd be tripping on every rock and tree branch.

I thought he might scold me for standing up to the Endurans, like he had when he found out I'd followed them into the woods. But he didn't. He remained strangely quiet and thoughtful, his jaw flexing and relaxing and flexing again.

What was going on in that beautiful head of his?

"Have you found out anything more about my dad?" I asked, suddenly remembering I'd asked him to look into it. "I mean—I know it's only been a day..."

"Hmmm," he said, the faraway look in his eyes sharpening into focus. "Oh, right. Yeah. I did, sort of. Don't get excited," he said, and I tried to tamper down the rush of blood in my ears, and the pounding of my pulse. "I wasn't able to learn much, but that's where I was last night. I left to make some inquiries."

So, that was why he never showed up. I'd have been lying if I said I hadn't thought of him in my pain and fever addled stupor. That I hadn't wished for him to come and be at my side. Hoped maybe just the sight of him might ease some of the pain.

"What did you learn?"

He held a branch away from us as we stepped over a thick, moss covered trunk and grasped my hand tightly to make sure I stayed upright. "Well, he was a," he began, hesitating before he spoke again, his voice apologetic and strained. "A figurehead of sorts. In the group of witches who want to reveal themselves to the humans. The radical group, *Manifesto.*"

They had a name for themselves? I wondered how many of them there were... but the more alarming thought running and stumbling through my mind, was the thought that my father was a radical in a group whose aim was to reveal witch-kind to humans. To reveal all the races to them, if I wasn't mistaken.

It seemed odd, but I thought perhaps that was only because I believed the exact opposite. I didn't agree with him, even though I wanted to.

Humans could not be trusted.

Humans were dangerous.

Hadn't history proven that time and time again? The fear of the unknown drove them to do horrible things. If something like a story in an old book could rally them to war, what would they do if they thought monsters lived among them? It would be chaos.

But, Alistair had been in love with a human woman—was love really enough to drive him to something so extreme?

"Are you sure?" I asked Elias, trying to roll the idea around more in my head. To make it make more sense to me.

He frowned. "I am. He even petitioned for a seat on the council, to give Manifesto a voice where it mattered, but he never got it. He died before they even had a chance to formally review his request."

"Well, do you know what happened to him?" I stopped, pulling Elias to a stop with me.

There was an apology written in the fine-print of his stare as he closed his other hand over mine. "I can't be sure. It's all hearsay." He hesitated, trying to dance around telling me what he'd heard.

I didn't care if he thought whatever it was wasn't worth repeating. I wanted to hear it. "Just tell me."

He removed his hand from mine and a chill snaked up my arm. The twilight brought with it an icy breeze that had me shivering. "From the sounds of it, the majority of people seem to believe he was murdered."

I want to say I was shocked. In total dismay of his words. But they only solidified a suspicion that had been slowly growing in my mind since over-hearing the Magistrate and Headmaster Sterling.

Something awful had happened to my dad. He was stolen away from me before I even had the chance to know him. I wanted to know why. "For his beliefs? Who would do that?"

"Who knows," he replied. "The Manifesto group is large and constantly growing, and cutting off it's head would only be a temporary solution. I don't really see the sense in it if that was the case... Sorry to be blunt. But then again, I suppose it could have been anyone who didn't agree with his views. We may never know."

But I knew who I thought it was. Or at least,

someone who knew something more about it. Sterling. I would just need to find out for myself, and prove it. Whoever murdered my father wouldn't go unpunished forever. One way or another, I'd find out what really happened. And why.

I tucked my hair away from my face, kicking at the ground. "That's ok. I just wish I knew more," I said innocently, offering him a wan smile. There was no need to involve him any more than I already had. If there was foul play at work here, I didn't want him digging into dark corners he couldn't dig himself out of.

"Thanks for looking into it."

"Of course."

We resumed walking through the trees in silence. My mind was racing. I was second-guessing myself. Questioning everything I'd learned. Leo used to tell me my curious nature and sharp mind would get me into the most trouble someday, if I didn't fall down a manhole first.

But before I started asking questions and doing some digging of my own, I had to be certain. And I had to be willing to accept the consequences. If whatever this was went as high up as the Magistrate at the very tippity top of the witchy food chain then I could be in for some very serious shit.

The uncertainty and anger roiled and churned

the magic within me. I couldn't stop the surge of the earth's energy from rushing into me, but it wasn't wild like in New Orleans. This much, I could tamper on my own. Keep it at a consistently rolling boil that wouldn't spill over. It wasn't without some effort, though.

Good thing I was used to it.

I could make out the place where the woods ended, and the academy grounds began a little ways ahead.

Elias squeezed my hand, and I gasped as he pulled me back from leaving the cover of the trees. I looked to where my hand was still wrapped tightly in his. The contact soothing and warm and exciting all at the same time. And then I glanced up and was floored at the rugged beauty of his face in the shadows.

Why was he looking at me like that?

"You really are extraordinary," he breathed. "I can feel the raw power coming off of you in waves." He paused, and the way his teeth ran over his bottom lip turned my knees to Jell-O. "It calls to my magic."

I gasped. So, it wasn't just me.

He *did* feel it, too! The bastard. Making me doubt myself.

I opened my mouth to say something sarcastic,

or was it going to be witty? I couldn't remember because one minute he was an arms length away and the next I had the divine pleasure of watching his resolve snap.

Before I could blink he'd pulled me to him, our bodies colliding only a millisecond before our lips.

His fingers traveled up my arm to cup the back of my head, tilting me up while he pulled me against him. I softened at his gentle caress. An exquisite ache forming behind my breastbone and some place deeper—more primal.

A small moan liberated itself from my chest, and my arms wrapped around him—hungry fingers tugging at his leather jacket to keep him close. His spice and wood smoke scent was downright intoxicating, and I couldn't get enough of him.

"Elias," I whispered, and he jolted, whimpering as though in pain before he pulled away... but only far enough to rest his forehead against mine. Our heaving, broken breaths mingled in the pine-scented air. My fingers still clutched the back of his jacket. I didn't want to ever let go.

"I've been wanting to do that for a while," he said between breaths in a whisper-soft voice, letting loose a throaty nervous laugh. "I'm sorry if I—"

"Shhh," I said, covering his mouth with my index and middle finger. He shivered. "You have nothing to be sorry for."

But the moment I said it, I felt his spine go rigid where my right hand still held a fistful of leather at his back. I watched his adams apple bob in his throat, and a crease form in his forehead. Why hadn't I just kept my damn mouth shut?

15

I was still in a stupor the next day when Bianca burst into our room just before dinner. After dealing with the Endurans in the woods, and processing Elias' kiss, I thought it would be a good idea to bury my nose in a book for a while and went to library. But it didn't matter how many pages I flipped through on familiar lore, and *man* was there a *lot* of it, I could find absolutely nothing on how to undo the binding magic.

And nothing even remotely interesting enough to evict the thoughts of Elias from my mind.

I chucked the book I'd brought back to my room with me to the other end of the bed, glad for a proper distraction. "Hey!" I said, trying to muster up a cheery voice. To shake off the million questions and confusing thoughts vying for my attention at the edges of my mind. "How was your visit?"

She dropped a couple of paper bags emblazoned with designer brand names down on her bed. I'd never seen her in regular clothes, I realized. But there she was in a bright yellow dress, with brown suede lace-up boots climbing her legs to her calves, and a purposefully faded jean jacket. She looked good.

"It was great! My little brothers just got one of those virtual reality video game things and they're, like, addicted to it, so I hardly got to spend any time with them. But I managed to get some shopping in, and a soak in the hot-tub."

Sounded glamorous. And here I was hiding out in our dorm room from the sidelong glances and outright stares of the other students as they returned from their weekends away. It seemed there were more than a few of them who believed I *was* in fact to blame for the freakish storm Friday night. *Ugh.*

I was about to ask her what she bought, when she gasped, whirling around to face me, her eyes wide and excited. "Oh! And I told them all about you—my brothers, I mean. They are dying to come into their powers, so when I told them I was roomies with the most powerful witch at the academy, they were all ears. They're super excited to meet you!"

I snorted. Ignoring the fact that she'd told them

I was pretty much a mega witch, which was *so* not true. A bit more powerful than most, maybe—but that was it. "Yeah well they'll be waiting..." I pretended to glance at an invisible watch on my wrist. "Oh about another four years before I can leave."

"Right," Bianca said, deflating as she chewed her bottom lip. "Hey! Why don't you just come with me? We have a guest room, or you can just stay with me in my room! Uncle Sterling never says no to me. We could go next weekend."

My first instinct was to say no, I didn't want to go anywhere near Headmaster Sterling's house—but, wait... that wasn't quite true, was it? I sucked in a breath.

Maybe it was exactly where I wanted to be. He could have council documents there. Or files. Or any manner of things that could lead me to finding out more about my dad. If I had something to hide, I wouldn't hide it in the academy, I'd keep it someplace private, like in my bedroom, or in a private office in my home. Somewhere no one else would stumble on it.

"Yeah," I said hastily. "Actually. I'd love that. Sounds fun."

She smiled wide, and sat down, pulling her designer shopping bags onto her lap. My own smile faltered, and an ugly, guilty feeling weighed down my shoulders and pressed on my chest.

I wanted to talk to her about my dad. To tell her what I learned, but then I would have to tell her I suspected her uncle had something to do with it. And, I didn't know exactly how close they were. Would she freak out? Tell him I was basically accusing him of harboring information, or worse, that I thought he might have actually had something to do with it?

That sure as hell wouldn't be getting me any brownie points. And I had to admit, there was a chance I could be completely wrong. *I'll tell her,* I told myself. *I'll tell her when I know for sure one way or the other.*

"So," she said, and I realized I hadn't been paying attention. I looked up and she was holding out two headbands. A navy blue lululemon one, and a simple black one like the one I was already wearing, except hers wasn't fraying at the edges and faded from years of use. "I noticed you had a thing for headbands."

She must've seen the thrill in my expression because she laughed and I squealed, jumping off the bed. I didn't think anybody had ever bought me anything, except for Leo and Lara, of course, but that was different.

I reached out to touch the navy one, the fabric

looked so soft, but I stopped just before my finger-tips could brush the fine fabric. "You really shouldn't have bought me anything," I said, realizing I wouldn't be able to return the favor. I hadn't so much as a dime to my name.

"They're headbands," she said with a mock look of annoyance. "It's not like I bought you a damned Bugatti. Take them! Yours is... well, it was in need of replacement."

I took them from her outstretched hands, immediately replacing the old ratty one I was wearing with the navy blue one. It fit snugly and held my hair firmly away from my face. "Thank you," I said, more than a little awkwardly.

"You're welcome," she said, tossing the other bags into the closet. "Now, shall we get some dinner? I'm starved."

IT TOOK Bianca four days to convince Sterling to let me go with her for the weekend, and when she told me earlier that afternoon I was shocked. Not like I doubted her or anything, but I really thought this was the one time her uncle may not give in to her every whim.

From what she told me, he was quite the doting parental figure. And I thought it so strange to think of him that way and not as the snake I thought he was.

"It's super weird, though—him saying we aren't allowed to leave the house. I really wanted to show you around," Bianca whispered, glancing up from the thick volume laid out in front of her on the wide wooden table between us. "I don't know why he'd say that."

We were in the library. The both of us studying for a big test in incantations tomorrow morning, when really I should have been doing more research. Trying to come up with something—anything to do what I told Cal and Adrian I would find a way to do.

"I can think of a reason or two," I blurted before I could stop the words from slipping out.

"What? What do you mean?"

I supposed it was alright if she knew the truth about that one thing. Now that I knew her, I felt fairly confident she wouldn't judge me.

"Well, you never really asked why I just randomly started coming to Arcane Arts Academy more than halfway through the term..."

Her brown eyes sparked with interest, and her mouth fell open. "Dish!" she ordered me, a little louder than was necessary.

The librarian, an older woman with a large bun of silver hair and horn-rimmed spectacles on a thin gold chain, hushed us sharply from the front of the enormous room.

She must've had supersonic hearing. The library was a castle unto itself, taking up almost an entire wing of the academy. It had shelves stacked floor to ceiling on the main floor, with rolling ladders for the students to reach the ones higher up. Two study areas, which was where we sat near the back, in the smaller one of the two. And an open second level with carved banisters so the people above could see down below and vice versa.

It was my favorite place in all of the academy— or at least it was until I'd had to start spending every free second of my time scouring hundreds of pages for information I wasn't even sure existed. I must've looked through over a hundred books since last Friday... and I had the papercuts to prove it.

"Harper!" Bianca urged. "Tell me!"

I leaned in over the table. "Alright! Just calm down. Quit being so damned loud. You're going to get us kicked out."

"Pffffft," she said. "Please. Have you forgotten whose uncle runs this place? Now, dish before I pry it from you. Pretty sure I just saw an incantation for that."

I gave her a snide look, rolling my eyes before the whole story began to pour from my lips like a faucet left wide open. I told her what happened in the market square at the French Quarter. About the unintentional earthquake I'd caused. And the kind council member who took pity on me, and sent me here instead of Kalzir, or some other awful place.

When I was finished, she sat back in her chair, her mouth hanging open. "It makes so much sense now," she said. "No wonder my uncle kept asking about you!"

"You didn't tell him, did you? About..." I said, my gaze flicking to the windows behind her and what waited for me out in the woods there. I gulped.

"Of course not," she said, looking only mildly offended.

I breathed. Relieved not to find a single trace of judgment in her eyes. She went back to studying like I hadn't just finished telling her I'd broken two of our laws and was basically sent here as a prison sentence. She was surprised, sure, that much was obvious. But no more than that.

It was official. She was starting to grow on me. With some weight taken from my shoulders, I felt lighter when I went back to studying. But within ten minutes the tome I had open in front of me started to blur together and I realized how incredibly tired I was. Not just tired of reading a million words in old, boring texts, but also tired of so many other things.

I unburdened myself of one tiny thing, but there was a herd of others stampeding through my head to take its place. I was tired of tests and failing in class. Tired of not being able to get a private second with Elias to talk about what happened between us in the woods. Tired of not being able to learn anything else about my dad or what happened to him.

Just. Plain. Tired.

"I don't think I've ever seen him in anything but a suit," Bianca said, breaking my focus, and I turned to follow her trail of vision, finding Elias on the other end. In his leather jacket and jeans.

What was he doing?

Our eyes locked for an instant, and his hands clenched, conveying a message of urgency. A moment later he turned and left. He needed to talk to me.

I whirled back around in my seat. Swallowed as I fought a blush and the racing of my pulse.

"I'd like to get to know *his* history, if you know what I mean," Bianca said, waggling her eyebrows and licking her lips. I stood so quickly my chair fell over behind me, crashing against the marble tile. I rushed to right it, mouthing an apology to the librarian who was shooting daggers at me with her eyes.

"I'm—uh—going to get a coffee. You want one?"

Bianca lifted one of her perfectly manicured

blond brows at me. "Yeah. Sure. Everything alright?"

I pushed my chair back in. "Just super tired. This test is going to be the death of me."

"Tell me about it," she laughed quietly. "Hurry back, though. We haven't even gotten to the chapter on the dangers of mispronunciation."

I nodded. *Yay.* I couldn't wait.

Squishing down the panic before it could do more than make my skin itch and a ball form in my throat, I rushed toward the exit after Elias. Weaving through the stacks to save myself some steps. That's where she caught me.

"Why in such a rush?" she asked from behind me and I froze, gritting my teeth as I spun on one heel. I'd admit, I fully expected some sort of retribution from the resident queen bitch, but I did *not* have time for this crap right now.

I turned to face her, and she flipped her yellow-blond hair away from her chest. There was one button too many undone on her blouse, revealing a lacy cream and black bra beneath. *Classy.*

"What do you want, Kendra?"

It was strange seeing her alone, and I immediately scanned the aisle of books, looking for her two minions.

"Me?" she asked, feigning apprehension. "Oh, nothing really," she continued, drawing out her vowels in that way people like her did when they wanted to sound super dramatic and mysterious. She was pulling off the dramatic bit, but I wasn't the least bit curious what she had to say.

She stepped in closer with her manicured hands clasped behind her back, her chin raised high. I glanced longingly at the exit, mere meters away from where Kendra and I now stood between two towering bookcases.

"I just had a question," she said, batting her lashes at me innocently, her voice so sickeningly sweet it made me want to barf.

"I don't have time for this," I snapped at her, stepping away. "I have studying to do."

I turned to leave.

"Is that what you were doing out in the woods the other night? Studying?"

My lips pressed together, and a clammy sweat sprang from my pores, coating my palms and the back of my neck. *Shit.* If I turned around and tried to make up an excuse, she'd know I was hiding something. I was a crap liar, and I knew it.

But if I didn't say anything, she might think she was onto something.

Oh no... had she seen me coming out of the woods with Elias?

The panic was starting to mount, and I bit the inside of my cheek hard enough to draw blood.

Racking my brain. Trying to come up with something to say. Grasping at slick straws.

No, she couldn't have seen us together. It was the weekend then. She wouldn't have been here. Almost nobody was. They'd all gone home to visit friends and family. At least that one secret was still safe.

For now.

I shuddered to think what would happen if it ever wasn't. I didn't want to think about the repercussions Elias could face. It made me feel selfish and cruel.

"I saw you come out of the trees looking a bit... disheveled. Meeting someone out there, were you? Not practicing magic off academy grounds, I hope," she continued, circling me. "Oh! Or maybe you were hoping to finally bond to your familiar. Did you know that you're the *only* one in the entire academy who doesn't have one? I checked."

Well then, she didn't check all that well, did she? Since I *did* have a familiar. I had *two* of the damned things. And I wasn't the only one who didn't have one. Both Sterling and one of the other teachers' familiars had passed on.

I wanted to scream at the unfairness of it all. What did she know, anyway? I'd give anything to go back to not having a familiar if it meant *not* being eaten alive by a pack of wolves.

My magic ignited within me as though she'd thrown a lit match into my gasoline filled veins. The floor beneath my feet trembled.

Stop, Harper. Reign it in.

I didn't need to draw any more attention to myself than I already had.

My fists shook with the effort of containing it. Kendra looked to the floor and back up to me, throwing out her hands for balance. Genuine surprise flashed across her features.

Good. I wanted her to see that I was stronger than her. I'd be damned if I stood there and let a spoiled brat like Kendra Van Damme try to scare me. I had much bigger problems to deal with.

I unclenched my fists and shouldered past her. "Why don't you come into the woods with me next time and find out," I hissed. Hoping to throw her off by offering to freely have her join me... and maybe to scare her—but only a little. If my wolves scared the piss out of her, it wouldn't be my fault.

I checked myself, stomping through the stacks Not *my* wolves. They weren't mine. Would never be mine.

I was still twitchy and fuming when I left the library, pushing down the swell of magic vying for release at my fingertips. I found Elias near the back exit, leaning against the stone wall with his head bent and brows furrowed.

He looked up when he saw me coming and kicked off from the wall to walk outside. I slowed, watching him descend the steps and head in the direction of his cabin. It was still daylight outside. I'd have to wait at least a few minutes before I followed him and then take a roundabout way of getting there to avoid any wandering eyes. Like the vile ones of Kendra.

Had he finally found something that could help us? With only one day left in my bargain with the Endurans, it would be a huge relief to have at least one of the problems checked off my ever-growing list. I counted to sixty in my head, bouncing from one foot to the other, before I exited the academy. I walked toward the woods, in the opposite direction of Elias' cabin, being extra cautious to check that no one else was outside or watching from the windows.

Once I was under the cover of the trees, I changed my path and cut back to where his cabin squatted at the southeast corner of the grounds. Smoke rose from the chimney, and he'd left the door open for me to come in. I hesitated. We hadn't had a chance to see much of each other outside of class since... since he kissed me.

My stomach did a little flip.

You're here now, Harper. Just go inside and see what this is all about.

I rushed inside, taking care to close the door

behind me. "Hey," I said when I found him standing by his kitchen sink, his hands braced on the counter.

He didn't turn around at first. It was almost like he was afraid to. But then he did, and I saw the crease was still in his forehead. It'd been there since the night he'd come to my aid in the woods. And it hadn't left. I was the cause of that crease.

"They're too quiet out there," he fumed, his hands grasping at the air around his sides. "I went looking for them," he added, and I was taken aback. He'd done what?

What if they'd torn him apart?

"But I couldn't find them, or any trace of their pack. They must be from really far away."

"Why did you go looking for them? What's going on?" I asked, my pulse peaking and dipping with spikes of adrenaline and pounds of compounded stress.

"It's what's *not* going on, Harper," he said with a harshness to the words I'd never heard him use before. His rubbed a rough hand over his face, and rubbed his eyes. "There's nothing."

"What?"

"There is no spell, sigil, or incantation to sever a witch familiar bond. I'm sorry. I tried." Defeat shone in his eyes, and made his gaze fall and his chest heave. I didn't think he was used to being defeated.

A large part of me wanted to scream and cry and melt into a puddle of tears. I had been so hopeful that there'd be a way to do it. To have that hope crushed was devastating, but not as devastating as the look on Elias' face. The guilt filling his jaw with tension. The shame dragging down the corners of his eyes and mouth. The fear and frustration making his hands shake.

I couldn't stand to see him like that.

I walked over to him and laid a hand on his chest, compelling him to lift his head. "We both knew there was a slim chance of it. We told them that, too. It'll be alright."

He shook his head. "It won't. Don't you see? They'll look for other ways to sever the bond. And if they won't do it themselves, when their alpha finds out, he will."

I stepped back. "Well then lets try what you suggested. Make a new spell for it."

He scoffed, dragging himself to the sofa. "You were right, it was a foolish idea. Too dangerous. It could backfire and you could be hurt. It isn't worth the risk."

"More dangerous than two Enduran shifters and possibly an entire pack? More dangerous than other people finding out?"

He bend his head over his knees and pressed his forehead into his palms, groaning. "I don't like this. It's driving me insane thinking you're in danger."

My breath caught. "I'm sorry you got dragged into this," I told him, walking over to stand in front of him at the side of the couch.

"I just want you to be safe."

I smirked. "I am for tonight, at least," I offered, doing my best to add a smile to the words. "And tomorrow if everything goes as planned, I'll be spending the night—well, the whole weekend, really, with my roommate at her house."

He cocked his head at me. "Bianca Matthews?"

I nodded. "Yeah, she invited me to stay over. I was hoping we'd have this figured out by tonight or early tomorrow before we left, but I guess I'll have to tell them we'll need more time."

I rebelled against the thought of telling them. How would they react? They'd be pissed.

"No!" he said in a rush, jumping back to his feet. "You won't tell them anything. I'll do it. I'll tell them."

I narrowed my eyes at him.

"Please. Let me talk to them. You go to Bianca's where they can't get to you. And then maybe... I don't know, maybe I can get them to see reason. To understand."

Yeah... right.

I needed to go to Bianca's. I couldn't refuse the

opportunity to find out what was going on with Sterling, and my father, and the Magistrate. But I didn't like the idea of leaving him to deal with the Endurans without me. When he told them we'd failed, they'd be angry. What if they lashed out at him?

"I'm stronger than them. More powerful. You don't have to worry about me," he said as if he'd read my thoughts.

I could see his mind was already made up, and I wouldn't argue. They wouldn't harm him without their alpha's permission. If they did and were caught, it would be seen as an act of war and their entire pack would pay for their mistake. No, they wouldn't hurt him. Not even the hot-headed Adrian would dare.

"Fine," I said after a few beats of tense silence looking into his pleading eyes. "But be careful. And don't provoke them."

He yanked me into an embrace. "Thank you," he said and I relaxed into him. Luxuriating in the feel of his arms around me. "I don't think I'm the one who needs reminding of that, by the way," he whispered against my hair. "But don't worry, I'll play nice."

I laughed into the leather of his jacket. Then I pulled back to look into his eyes. My magic reached out to him, and I leaned in with it. But he pulled away, and a troubled frown stained his lips. "Good," he said in a gruff voice. "Glad that's settled."

I wanted so badly to ask him why he still fought it, but I didn't want to push him and risk him using the momentum to keep moving further away from me. But I had to wonder if he thought what he did in the woods was a mistake? I didn't want to believe that, or that the connection between us was somehow *wrong*.

"I'll walk you back to the academy," he said, moving toward the door, and it was like someone dumped ice-water into my blood.

And people said women were the ones who didn't know what they wanted. *Ha!* What a joke.

I stepped past him. "I'll walk myself."

He didn't try to stop me, but I never heard his front door close.

"I completely bombed that test," I whined to Bianca when we came out of incantations that afternoon.

I tried to focus on studying when I finally got back to the library, but my mind was elsewhere— like on the way Elias' hair shone with bits of copper in the firelight of his hearth. How he always rubbed his jaw when he was flustered, as though exhausted by whatever plagued his mind. And then of course, there were the other things. The less pleasant thoughts. About sharp-toothed wolves and snake-like men.

It didn't help that in history class right before incantations, Elias had all but completely ignored me, even though I raised my hand twice to answer his questions. He'd chosen others. Was I being stupid?

Yeah, I'm probably being stupid.

But I couldn't help it.

"Well, maybe if getting coffee hadn't taken you nearly an hour then you'd have had more time to study," Bianca said in a told-you-so tone. "What'd you do, get lost?"

I lifted one shoulder in a half shrug. "Sort of." I sighed, hefting my books higher in my arms, my stomach in knots at the thought of eating lunch. "When are we leaving?" I asked, changing the subject to something more promising.

Bianca flashed me her winning smile, and I could tell she was immeasurably excited to have someone to bring home with her. I didn't think she had many friends at the academy, either. "Right after class if we can swing it!"

When I thought about it, I hadn't seen her do more than wave to a few other students or say hi. And she mostly only did that when the 'student' in question was a beautiful African American guy named Marcus. He had come-hither eyes, lips that looked pillow-soft, and some of the best cheekbones I'd ever seen on a man. If I hadn't noticed Bianca's interest in him, I'd have been drooling over him, too.

We passed him in the hall and Bianca lengthened her strides, and her hips swayed a little more than they did normally. She had it *bad*. "Are you ever going to actually talk to him, or are you just going to stare at him forever?"

She gasped, jumping as though stung. "Shut up," she squeaked, adding, "He could've heard you," when we were further away, glancing back to watch him as he rounded the corner back toward the male dorms. Funny, I never took her as being shy.

"I'll talk to him," she said. "When the time is right."

"And by that you mean when you manage to grow a pair of lady balls?"

Two other girls walking near us swiveled their heads, shooting us looks that managed to be shocked and disgusted all at once, before they migrated further away.

"Harper!" Bianca scolded, herding me into the cafeteria as if I was an ox in need of prodding. "Don't you have even the smallest filter?"

I pouted. Shook my head. "Mmmmm, no, don't think so."

She rolled her eyes, dragging me behind her to the serving line, muttering. "Of all the roommates…"

. . .

In Bianca's borrowed jeans that were a size too big for my non-existent booty, and three inches less of height, as well as a borrowed soft black turtleneck, we rushed through the hallways toward the staff wing.

It felt weird wearing her clothes, but when I told her all I had were the ratty old jean shorts and tank top she first saw me in, she had insisted, saying I couldn't wear my uniform off academy grounds because *that's just sad.*

I was inclined to agree. I couldn't wait to get out of the damn thing. The blouses were particularly uncomfortable, always coming back from the laundry too stiff and starched.

"It really is too bad your feet are so big," Bianca said to me with a smirk. "I'd have leant you some leather boots that would've looked killer with that sweater."

Heeled boots, I was sure. "Yeah, too bad," I said sarcastically. Anything more than a two-inch heel and it would be downright dangerous for anything in my immediate surroundings. Even two inches might've been pushing it. "Think I'll stick to my flip flops."

She snickered at me and urged me to hurry up with jerk of her head. "Come on, Uncle Sterling doesn't like to be kept waiting." She sped up, struggling with the awkward weight of Blanche in her arms. The rabbit watched me with her unnerving red eyes, looking painfully bored with the whole situation.

"What? I thought we were portaling out ourselves?"

"Nah. He insisted on escorting us. I'm sure we have your criminal record to thank for that."

Ugh.

"At least we don't have to wait in line to use the portaling room. It takes over an hour sometimes if you don't get there straight after class. My uncle's office is the only other place in the building you can portal into and out of unless you go beyond the wards."

I bit my cheek and rubbed the bit of sweat on my palms off on my borrowed jeans. "Will he be home this weekend?" I asked, my voice coming out higher pitched than I'd intended.

She tucked her wavy blond hair behind her ears. "Probably not. He usually has council stuff to attend to on the weekends. He only really comes home to sleep, if he does at all. It'll just be us and my brothers—oh, and Pierre, but he's like a ghost. You won't even notice him."

"Pierre?"

"Security," she explained. "And there are a few servants, and the boys' nanny. But they all keep to themselves. None of them have ever ratted me out for anything."

I wondered what they would've ratted her out for? Aside from the flask she kept in her vanity, and the odd curse word when we were alone, Bianca seemed pretty tame. But then again, I was sure I seemed pretty tame, too, until I was ready to tackle a guy for trying to steal a few pieces of jewelry.

But that was different. I lived by a set of very simple rules; mess with me, I'll tell you off. Mess with my family, and all bets are off. I supposed now that I had someone to call a friend, it would now be 'friends and family'.

I hurried to keep pace with Bianca as she cut around the last corner and walked up to her uncle's door. "Ready?" she asked.

"Let's go."

She pushed the door open, not bothering to knock. "Uncle Sterling," she called, walking through the modestly sized waiting area and up to the main door of his office. I had been in such a rush to get away the first time I'd been in his office, that I neglected to even notice the little waiting area between one door and the other.

"Yes, come in." We heard him call from the other side of the closed door, and Bianca strolled inside with me lagging a few feet behind her.

Headmaster Sterling had just finished writing

something down on a sheet of paper at his desk, and he flipped it over as we entered so it was blank side up. "Ready to get going?" He asked, flashing Bianca his teeth in what could only be described as something halfway between a smile and a grimace, rising from his seat.

"We are," Bianca replied. "Thanks again," she added. "For letting Harper stay the weekend with me."

Sterling narrowed his eyes at me, and beneath his salt-and-pepper beard I saw his jaw twitch. "Of course, my dear. I know the both of you will be on your best behavior," he said, looking at me pointedly.

I bowed my head, the discomfort settling over me like a mist of ichor.

"We will," Bianca trilled, elbowing me in the ribs.

"Yes," I grunted. "We will."

Sterling moved to a blank space of wall behind his desk. "Then let's get you two on your way."

Bianca gave me a reassuring look, and bumped her shoulder against mine as we made to move into place behind her uncle. Headmaster Sterling cast the sigil to open the portal and drew the lines for the doorway around it. His magic was strong, and the swirling lines of the sigil glowed a strong, vibrant gold.

The portal opened up in a matter of seconds. The ornate wallpaper faded away to reveal a grand entryway with parquet floors, a spiral staircase, and a chandelier dripping crystals from the ceiling.

Bianca must've seen my mouth fall open because she laughed and said. "Wait'll you see my room."

Sterling moved aside for us to go through. I stuck close to Bianca's side as my feet stepped from plush carpet to cold, hard tile. "You're not coming?" she asked him, disappointment making her words low and clipped. More a statement than a question.

He tucked his hands behind his back and looked down at her. "I have too much to see to this evening. But I'll do my best to join you for dinner."

She nodded solemnly. "Alright."

I truly hoped for her sake that he had nothing to do with what happened to my father. That he wasn't the monster I thought he might be underneath it all. Bianca wasn't the type who would fare well as an orphan if her uncle was ousted from the council and sent to Kalzir. What would even happen to her? To her brothers?

I couldn't think about that. Knowing the truth had become a necessity. I *needed* to know how my father died, and if the person—or *people* responsible were brought to justice. Even if it was Bianca's uncle, I couldn't let him get away with it just to save her some misfortune, could I?

In a perfect world, I wouldn't have to worry about such things. But our world was far from perfect, and I tended to be exposed to the most flawed parts of it. As though I was made to withstand the harder things in life. Cut from some other cloth.

Sterling did another one of his smile grimaces and sealed the portal, leaving us staring at the inside of a front door that was double my height and wider than my reach if I extended both arms as far as they'd go. This was not a place for a street rat. But, I supposed... that wasn't what I was anymore.

I was a student at the prestigious Arcane Arts Academy. And Bianca Matthews was my friend.

"Show me around?" I asked her with a note of impatient excitement, already wondering which of the many hallways led to her uncle's office.

She set Blanch down with a pat on her head, and the fat rabbit hopped away. Bianca swept her arm in a wide arc over the grand parlor, allowing the disappointment to fall away from her expression like dead skin, making room for one of her brilliant white smiles. "Please, do follow me," she said in a mock British accent, and I laughed at her ridiculousness.

Bianca dragged me through all twelve-thousand

square feet of the mansion. Showing me the staffed kitchen that smelled of fresh spring greens and herbed butter, the library, the sitting room, the drawing room, and the family room. Those last three all looked the same to me aside from the color of the furniture.

There was also a dining room on the main floor, and an exit leading out to a tennis court and a pool inside an enclosure that was a monstrosity of glass. The light reflected off it was near blinding. Up the wide, curving staircase were the bedrooms. She gestured down the hallway to the left at the landing. "Uncle Sterling's bedroom and private office are down there," she said and I made a mental note.

"My brothers are in the loft apartment," she said and gestured to a narrower staircase leading up to yet another level. I could hear the *pew pew* of video game gunshots, and a young man groaned as he was obviously shot, blaming the game for being so *damned* laggy.

"I'll take you up to meet them in a minute," she said, grabbing my forearm to drag me the rest of the way down the hall. "I want to show you something."

I was in awe of her room, blinded by the brilliant white of the walls and fuzzy white carpets. As my eyes adjusted, I saw that the white was interspersed with shiny black decor and soft pink fabrics.

A bright yellow bedspread adorned her king-size bed. A mountainous pile of black and pink pillows atop it.

There was an ensuite bathroom to my right. A walk-in closet to my left. And a balcony at the other end of the cavernous room.

"Come see," she said, and I followed her out to the balcony. The moment she opened the door, the breeze blew in warm steam and I peered outside to find an enormous scoop of water suspended in the air outside the door. The water roiled and bubbled gently.

A magical hot-tub. Of course, she had a magical hot-tub. Why wouldn't she?

"My uncle did it for me a few weekends ago. I asked him for one of those glass-bottom ones that the humans have, but he made me this instead, isn't it awesome?"

I gulped, clutching onto the doorframe. There was no deck. No sides or railings. No... bottom. I looked down through the water, finding the stone walkway twenty feet below the where the water ended.

"Won't you fall through?" I asked Bianca, wary. My stomach doing backflips.

"Of course not," she chided. "Come on, I think I have a bathing-suit that'll fit you."

She did have one, but it was too small in the

chest, and too big on the bottom. It did the trick, though. And after hyperventilating for the first five or so minutes, I found the weird magical hot-tub wasn't all that terrifying after all.

If you pushed your feet too deep into the water, near the bottom, it would move lower, expanding to fit your added length. Making it effectually bottomless.

And, salty? The water was a strange consistency and made us more buoyant than normal. We could float at the surface without doing any awkward paddling or holding onto the ledge of her door frame. As the sun fell over their property and painted the back garden in hues of orange and pink, I felt all my tensions beginning to release.

I wanted to just *be* in the moment. Not worrying about tomorrow—or later tonight when I would sneak away after Bianca fell asleep—or anything else. It was just us, the hot roiling water, and the decanter of bourbon Bianca swiped from the dining room.

"So, what do you think? Glad you came?" Bianca asked after a while.

I sighed, sinking a little lower into the steamy water, being careful not to look down. Every time I did, I felt a wave of vertigo threaten to tip me over.

Heights and I didn't play nicely together. "Very,"

I replied, feeling more hair slip free of the loose red bun I'd piled atop my head.

Sitting back up, I looked out over the property, realizing I hadn't the slightest clue where we were. "Where is this? Are we still in West Virginia?"

Bianca followed my gaze. "No, we're in Oregon. That mountain over there is Mt. Hood. Portland is a couple hours' drive that way."

"And I'm assuming you don't have any neighbors out here," I said, thinking how if mortals saw a giant floating ladle-full of water, they might have a few questions.

She laughed, tipping the rest of her bourbon down her throat. "No, but it's warded, see," she said, pointing out into the distance. And if I squinted hard and focused, I could just make out the light shimmer of the dome covering their entire property.

Wow.

I knew some witches warded their homes, but it was usually only for short periods of time, and the wards would never be that large. They must have a power source somewhere in the house that it could draw constant energy from.

We learned that at the academy. How they imbued the very stones used to build it with conduit magic. They acted much the same as solar panels do. Except they got their energy from all the magical bodies in the academy, sucking up whatever little bits we exuded, and directed the power where it was most needed—mostly the wards.

Effectively, the building protected itself. Which was pretty darn cool.

It must've been nice, though. Growing up in a place where you wouldn't have to hide your magic. Using it whenever you wanted. Being able to practice. Not having to hold all that wild energy inside of you all the time.

"That's must take a lot of power," I mused.

She shrugged, frowning. "It's a luxury given to all council members," she said with a note of distaste, pouring herself another fingers width of bourbon. "All the council members' places of residence are warded like this. Perks of the job, I guess."

"You don't get to see him much, do you?"

"No. Not in the last few years anyway," she said, taking a sip. "We used to do all kinds of things together. He taught me how to ride." She pointed to what looked to be a stable far off in the distance. "And how to swim."

"What changed?"

Her steeped tea eyes met mine, and the corners of her mouth pulled down into a fleeting frown. "Beats me," she said.

"Heads up!" Someone shouted from inside

Bianca's room, and I looked up just in time to kick myself back before two boys took a running jump into the hot tub. Water sprayed up in their wake, stinging my eyes with salt.

"Your brothers, I assume?" I said from the edge of the tub before their heads poked back up.

Bianca cuffed them both on the back of the head. "Dimwits!" she chided them. "I thought I told you not to come in my room without asking."

"But you didn't tell us she was here!" one of them whined.

The boys were about thirteen. Maybe fourteen. they'd be coming into their powers any time now. They had the same golden blonde hair as their sister, the same slender frames, and warm brown eyes. They couldn't have been any more than a year apart in age.

"I'm so sorry," Bianca said. "These are the two nitwit brothers I told you about. He's Louie," she said pinching his cheek. "And he's Eddie. The two biggest pains in my ass."

Completely ignoring their older sister, the two of them turned their attention to me.

"Is it true you can make lightning come down from the sky," the one called Eddie asked.

"Can you show us?" Louie asked, turning back to his sister. "B, make her do it!"

I rolled my eyes playfully and finished the rest of

my bourbon in one long, burning swallow. "Your sister is a liar. I can do no such thing."

Bianca stuck her tongue out at me and shoved her little brothers back toward the edge of the tub. "Now get out! Both of you. And dry your feet before you go walking through my room. *Damned heathens.*"

17

We snacked on a platter of fruit, cheeses, and salty meats after we'd finished in the hot tub. We chatted. Changed into pajamas and bathrobes. It took a while, but I started to notice the things in her room that made it more than just a magazine cut-out.

An alternative rock band poster on the back of her closet door.

Chocolate bars in her nightstand.

And some weird creature that looked be out of some obscure anime as a stuffed animal hidden within the mountain of pillows on her bed.

Which is where she was now, fast asleep. After we'd stuffed ourselves, the bourbon started to drag down her eyelids and I was glad I'd only had the one glass. She was out in the matter of a few minutes. Leaving me sitting there, antsy and chewing on the inside of my cheek.

The house had been quiet for a long while. And earlier Bianca had told me the staff left every evening a few hours after supper. That only Pierre, the bodyguard, remained. And he generally patrolled the grounds so he could sneak cigarettes whenever he liked.

No one would dare launch an attack on a council member, she'd said, and I'd agreed. But wasn't that *exactly* what I was planning to do?

Just a quick look. Nobody is around to see me go in or come out. Just a peek, and then I'll go to sleep. Easy as pie.

Or was it cake?

I shook my head and slipped off the poofy moccasin-like slippers Bianca had given me to wear. They were hard-bottomed and would make too much noise against the hardwood in the hallway. Barefoot would be better.

My heartbeat pounded in my ears and the bourbon soured in my stomach. But I pressed on, looking back at Bianca's sleeping form. Her half-open eyes and gaping mouth. She wouldn't wake up.

I slipped out from the room, careful to turn the doorknob so the catch wouldn't click closed. I eased it in, letting the knob turn slowly in my palm.

Step one, complete, I thought to myself. *I've exited the room.*

Just a few more steps and then you're done. See? This is so easy.

Step two, creep down the hallway like a panther. *No, not like an elephant. Jesus.*

Ok. Step three, figure out which freaking room is Sterling's office.

There were two doors at the other end of the hallway. One at the very end and one on the left. I tried the one at the very end first. The breath sticking in my throat when the floor creaked beneath my feet.

A door closed somewhere downstairs, and I gasped, throwing myself into the room. My hands shook trying the shut the door without a sound. I held my breath, listening for a minute before deciding it must've just been Pierre coming in for a drink, or something.

He had no reason to suspect I'd be doing anything but sleeping, right?

Unless Sterling told him I was a felon and to keep an eye on me... the thought didn't help.

The inside of the room was dark and smelled faintly of sweet cigar smoke, and musk. I drew the sigil for light in the air over the door. The shape a waving line with a circle at the bottom. "Lucidus," I whispered, and the sigil glowed brighter. Amplified by the incantation.

Step three, complete. I found the office.

Even more ornate than his office at the academy, Sterling's home office was twice the size. Tall filing cabinets lined the wall to the right, and bookcases lined the wall opposite it. There was a small sitting area, and behind that was a long desk that looked to be at least a hundred years old if not more. A cold hearth sat empty and gray on the same wall as the cabinets, closer to the door.

I swallowed. Squeezed my hands into fists.

I'd better start looking.

18

My light sigil followed me as I made my way over to the filing cabinets. I found them all to be locked. *Crap.* I hadn't thought of that. I tried to remember the sigil to open locked things. Was it a V-like shape with a cross through it?

No, that wasn't right.

My stomach knotted. I tried to quiet my mind, remembering back to Ms. Granger's lessons the week before. We'd gone over this sigil. I could almost picture her drawing it on the board.

Wait, yes, I'd messed it up. It was a diamond with a curving shape inside of it and a line down the middle. That had to be it. And the incantation was...

Think!

My eyes flew open. I scrawled the symbol into

the air, and it glowed faint green. I channeled more power into it, knowing the spell would need to be strong to break whatever locking magic held the drawers shut.

Pressing my palm against the sigil, I spoke the incantation. "Resigno," and was rewarded with the falling domino sound of locks clicking open across all the cabinets.

I smiled. He obviously didn't see the need in using that strong of a spell in his own home. His mistake.

I pulled open the first drawer, my heart sinking at what looked like hundreds of files inside. And that was just one drawer. I called the light sigil to come closer and saw that at the very least, the folders seemed to be categorized in alphabetical order.

Looking under 'A' for Alistair, I found nothing. It took me two tries to find the drawer that held the files for 'H', but there was nothing there either. Not under 'Harper' or 'Hawkins'.

Frantic, I started looking through all the files, not wanting to come up empty-handed. There had to be something here. I didn't go through all this— leave Elias alone to deal with Cal and Adrian, *and* lie to my friend just to find absolutely nothing.

There were files for Arcane Law, and a whole bunch of trials and the official sentencing for each one. There were files on each of the council members. On finances. And even on investigations. And... Manifesto.

That file was thick. The edges worn. I pulled it out and set it atop the others, flipping it open. Inside, at the very top of the pile was a photo of a man with dark hair and green eyes. He was tall and wore a long pea-coat. I didn't think he knew the photo was being taken by the way he looked over his shoulder.

A gold ring circled his index finger. The design a bird with a golden eye.

All the breath whooshed from my body, and my hands shook as I lifted the photo up, tilting it into the light. It was him, I was sure of it. My father, Alistair Hawkins. And if I wasn't sure, when I lifted the photo, beneath it I caught a scribble of red ink that told me so.

I stuffed it into the pocket of my borrowed pajamas. I could agonize over it later, I thought, swallowing down the urge to cry. I had to hurry. I was fairly sure Bianca wouldn't be waking up anytime soon, but I couldn't be sure.

And Headmaster Sterling hadn't returned for dinner, but that didn't mean he wouldn't return at all. Though it was doubtful at this late hour.

I flipped through the documents, finding information on possible hideouts. Possible plans. More pictures of other witches who formed the radical group. But there was nothing to indicate foul play. Unless you counted the word 'eliminated' scrawled over a sheet that held my father's description.

And then I noticed something I hadn't before; on the same page in a block of text describing my father's role in the group was a blacked-out block of words. The beginning of the sentence read: *It's possible Hawkins attained sensitive information pertaining to* —but the rest was completely blacked out.

What had he found out?

I flipped through more pages. More files. But I found nothing. If the clock atop his mantle was to be trusted, I'd already been in his office for an hour. I couldn't risk staying much longer.

The desk! I hadn't checked the desk. I snapped my fingers for my sigil to move faster as I ran over to the large mahogany monstrosity. There were several drawers in each side, and I rushed to check each one, checking for trap doors or secret compartments... feeling a bit silly when I didn't find any.

All that was inside was quills and ink and a half a bottle of brandy and some cigars. Atop the desk were stacks of documents and...

The words appeared on the sheet of parchment before my eyes. My skin tingled and my hairs stood up straight on my arms. My breaths came fast and ragged as I watched the message come through from whoever sent it from the parchment's twin.

Someone else is asking questions now. A man at Sigilante last week.

The writing paused, and I wracked my brain to remember that Sigilante was a tavern. A witch's tavern warded against mortals.

Yet another professor from your Academy, I am led to believe.

I gasped. *Elias!* How did they found out he was asking about my dad? *Fuck!* Why had I asked him to go digging? Idiot!

Find out who he is. This is your mess, Atticus. Clean it up. We can't afford any loose ends. He knows something. Either dispose of him, or I'll have no choice but to resort to my own methods of dealing with this situation.

Dispose of him? I bit my clenched fist to keep from whimpering. From screaming. My chest ached and my stomach heaved. I swallowed back the bile that tried to creep up my throat.

I had to get back to the academy. *Now.* I had to warn Elias. He had to run. To get as far away from the council's reach as he could. Would I ever see him again? The thought made me clutch my chest. My magic rioted in my core.

This is all a bad dream. They couldn't kill Elias, could they? They'd never get away with it. What was so important that they'd kill someone just for asking questions about it?

Glancing back down at the desk, I noticed a half-drunken glass of amber liquid. And a cigar in an ashtray—only partially smoked.

The floor outside the door to the room creaked. I froze.

The handle turned and I shuddered. A hundred neurons fired in my brain all at once and I was overwhelmed. I didn't know what to do. Run? Hide? My magic crashed against the shores of my skin. Waiting for me to unleash it.

A heartbeat before the door opened, I broke free from the shell of terror rooting me to the spot. I swiped through my light sigil and plunged the room back into darkness. Then, as the door began to yawn open, I snatched the parchment from the top of the desk and threw a ward over myself, thick as a down duvet. Strong as iron.

I willed the ward to stay with me. To move as I did. I'd never had to form a moving ward before and sweat broke out over my brow with the concentration I needed to keep it in place.

The lights flicked on, blinding me, and I clamped my mouth tightly shut and slapped my free hand over it to stop the sounds of my shaking breaths.

Sterling stared straight at me, and I clenched the

parchment in my fist tighter, the paper making a crumpling sound that was the loudest thing I thought I'd ever heard.

And then he looked away, sighing. Removing his outer coat to hang it on a rack beside the door.

It'd worked! My ward held. He couldn't see me. I focused harder, maintaining the steady flow of energy I allowed to leak out from my pores to keep it nice and strong. I had to get out of there... If he paid any closer attention, he could sense my presence, and if I made any sudden movements, he could catch sight of my ward.

I removed my hand from my mouth and licked my lips. The parchment in my grasp felt like a red-hot poker. Burning into my skin. What would he do when he noticed it was gone?

I mirrored his movements, trying to make my way to the door. For each step he took toward his desk, I took one more toward the door, holding to my ward for dear life. My heart beat wildly, painfully. Beating at the bones of my ribcage like a wrecking ball against brick.

He stepped. I stepped. He moved to the right. I moved to the left.

My ward started to waver, and I panicked, stumbling over the coffee table in the sitting area as I tried to move backward through the room. I went down *hard* against the oriental rug, dragging what remained of the ward down with me.

I flipped over quick as a cat, spinning to face him on all fours. He cocked his head at the space right above where I crouched low between the oversized armchairs. Then he raised his thick dark brows and fell into the chair at his desk.

He was going to notice. He would see the parchment was missing and I would be done for. I scrambled to the door, cursing under my breath.

Now, what, Harper? He'd closed the door behind him, and I couldn't very well open it. He'd definitely notice that. And my ward would break down any second. I couldn't hold it much longer. It didn't matter how strong my magic was if I didn't have the skill to hold it in place.

Sterling lit his cigar, and a cloud of white-gray smoke puffed around his face. My whole body was covered in icy cold sweat, and the nausea was starting to come back. I was going to have to open the door. It was the only option.

"Pierre!" Sterling shouted suddenly, and I clamped my hands back over my mouth, inching back away from the door.

Eight seconds later, the door opened, and Pierre stepped into the room.

"Go check on the girls," he said, and I didn't

dare move. If I did, he'd see the shimmer of my ward, I was certain of it.

I watched him like a hawk, waiting for him to look away. For them both to look away, only for a second. I just needed one damned second. Please.

Please.

"They're asleep. Have been for a while," Pierre responded.

Sterling looked at him as though he was the daftest person he'd ever beheld. "Go check on them," he ordered his hired man in an annoyed tone, waving his cigar through the air as though it were a marshaling wand and he was directing a plane. "My niece's room is that way. Go!" he added when Pierre didn't make a move.

And then Sterling looked back down at his desk, and Pierre turned away.

I bolted out the door, nearly tripping in my haste to make it down the hall, praying neither of the men could hear my thunderous footfalls through the walls of my weakened ward. I slid into Bianca's room and sealed the door behind me, running for the bed.

I released the ward, tucked the parchment beneath my pillow, and crawled under the covers. Sealed my eyes shut.

The door clicked back open and Pierre stepped inside. The door closed again a minute later, once he was satisfied at having seen us both fast asleep. I waited with bated breath until I heard his footfalls descend the stairs, and the soles of his shiny shoes hit the marble tile.

I whirled on Bianca, shaking her shoulders. Her mouth closed, and she squeezed her eyes closed, moaning.

"What?" she whined, trying to turn away from me. "Go back to sleep, dude. I was having such a good dream."

"Wake up," I said, and something in my tone must've gotten her attention because she slowly rolled back toward me and peeled her eyes open. The only light in the room was from a softly glowing orb hovering above her bedside table. She reached out and touched it, making it glow brighter with the addition of her magic.

When she saw my face, all traces of sleepy, whiny Bianca vanished. She sat up, looking around the room as though there might be monsters crawling on the floor or up her walls. "What is it? Has something happened?"

I didn't know what to say. Sorry, but your uncle is the Magistrate's murderous henchman, and he's after a teacher I may or may not be in love with? Dammit all to hell! She would think I was insane.

"I need you to portal me back to the academy,"

I said in a rush, never breaking eye contact with her. "Now."

She kicked the covers from her legs and stood, pulling her housecoat back on. Her wavy blonde hair stuck up at all angles and her mascara was smudged. "What's happened? You're freaking me the fuck out, Harper."

I had to give her something. "There's someone in danger at the academy," I blurted. "I—I can't say anything else yet. Just please, *please* portal me back."

I'd have done it myself if I was confident I remembered the sigil, but even if I did remember it, I didn't know the portal spots in the house. I knew there was one somewhere around the front door, but we'd never make it down there without being heard or caught.

"You have to tell me what's going on!" she nearly shouted.

"Shhhhhh," I said, ready to leap on her to keep her quiet if I had to.

"If someone is in danger at the academy, I have to tell my uncle. He can help us."

"No, he can't!" I said, my throat feeling as though it was about to close up. The anxiety mounting to something I soon wouldn't be able to control. "He *is* the danger."

Her mouth fell open, and she staggered a step

back as though I'd struck her. "What the hell is that supposed to mean?"

I reached under my pillow and yanked the parchment out, stomping the few steps until I was right in front of her. I thrusted it into her stomach, and she fumbled to grab it. "What is th—"

"Read it," I said, and fifty pounds of fury fell from my body, replaced with something much more ugly. Bianca wouldn't be able to unsee what she read. I'd explain it all to her. What they were talking about, and what it meant, but first she needed to do as I asked and get me out of here.

Her lips pursed and she glanced from the parchment, and back up to me. She shoved it back into my hands. "There's nothing on here."

She was right. The words had vanished. *No!* Sterling must've realized it'd been taken... which meant he'd have the real message by now and could already be on his way to the academy.

My eyes brimmed with tears. "If you won't help me then at least show me the sigil, I *have* to get back," my voice broke near the end, and I saw her resolve waver. "Please, Bianca."

She shook her head, exasperated, angry, and probably confused. I felt awful for putting her in this position. But I didn't have a choice. I hoped one day she'd see that, even if I didn't get the chance to explain it all. I had to believe she wasn't in danger.

He wouldn't go so far as to hurt his own niece, would he? Maybe it was better if she didn't know.

If she never found out.

She could go back to having our room to herself. Back to being blissfully unaware of the world outside her warded dwellings. It was only a matter of time until Sterling figured out I was the one who intercepted his message. If he hadn't already.

I couldn't stay at the academy anymore either.

My chest ached and an image of Cal and Adrian flashed behind my eyelids. What would I tell them?

Bianca bit her bottom lip and groaned, lowering her brows. Her balled hands trembled at her sides. "Alright, *fine*. Come with me."

19

When I'd refused to portal out the way we'd come in and told her we couldn't be seen, Bianca had grumbled, but relented. Then she'd led me into her closet and parted a rack of clothing near the back.

She told me her uncle would kill her if he found out she'd managed to tear a hole in the ward just to duck into and out of her closet.

I wanted to tell her she could be right, but I kept my mouth shut instead.

We stepped through and into the portaling room of the academy. The same space they used for making calls during the school week. It was dark and quiet. And I realized it would be a few hours later in West Virginia. We'd left Oregon around eleven in the evening, so, here it had to be closer to two o'clock in the morning.

Everyone would be asleep. Good. There was only one person I'd have to wake up.

"Thank you," I said to Bianca, as she closed the portal behind us. "You should go back before they notice you're gone."

She crossed her arms over her fluffy white housecoat and stared me down. "No, I'm staying," she replied stubbornly. "If you would tell me what's going on I might be able to help you, you know."

I gave her an impish smirk. "Not with this, you can't. Just stay inside. And when I come back in, I'll explain everything."

"You're going *outside* right now? Does this have something to do with your familiars? Is someone trying to hurt them?"

I had already started to back away; afraid Sterling would show up here any second—that he could *already* be here. "I'll be back as soon as I can," I muttered, ignoring her questions, and then turned and sprinted from the room.

Guilt pressed down on me. The pressure near bone-cracking. She deserved better than a friend who lied to her. Than an uncle who was a murderer.

I took the stairs two at a time, realizing I was barefoot a second before my feet connected with the earth. A sharp rock dug into my heel, but I kept moving, grunting through the throbbing ache.

I looked back at the academy as I went, checking for light or movement. I saw nothing.

The words I'd seen on the parchment drove me to go faster. The black ink scrawl branded into my subconscious. *We can't have any loose ends... dispose of him...*

With any luck, Sterling didn't yet know who the man in the tavern was. There were at least twelve other male professors at the academy. It could just as easily have been them, right? I had no reason to think he'd automatically suspect Elias.

But that wasn't right. I could feel it all the way down to the marrow in my bones. He was in danger. My blood surged with anticipation. My magic was already flaring up in defense.

Trust your gut, Leo had always told me. *It's the only thing you can trust in this messed up world.*

I never knew just how right he was.

It was instinct driving me, and I heeded its warning. Rose to it's primal cries. *Almost there now.*

I spotted his cabin through the trees. There was a subdued glow against the window pane. And smoke still rose from the chimney, though it was thin and gray. I didn't bother trying to be quiet as I sprinted up the front steps and banged on the door.

I tried the handle, but it was locked. "Elias!" I called through the wood. "Elias, are you in there?"

Listening closely, I heard a rustling sound, and then the relieving sound of footsteps coming toward the door. He released the lock and the door opened. I pushed my way inside, and shut the door behind me, peering out into the dark to make sure I wasn't followed.

I threw the bolt back into place and let loose a long breath that came out sounding more like a tempered sigh. *I made it.* I rested my head against the rough grain of the wood, taking a couple deep, calming breaths before I turned to face him.

When Elias still didn't say anything, I turned around, perplexed by his silence. "We need to talk," I said, and then I looked up and my heart stopped. Everything stopped.

And then my heart beat once, hard. And then again, harder. My magic raced to fill my blood, the buzzing warmth radiated through my entire body.

"Yes," said Headmaster Sterling, holding Elias in place with one hand, while an orb of glowing amber light flickered and pulsed in his other. The sigil at the heart of the orb glowed bright and strong. It was a complex symbol, and something about it made my stomach drop. It was all hard angles. Sharp lines and curving edges. "We should talk."

It was an attack spell, but I had no idea which one. We wouldn't learn those until after we turned eighteen... but judging by the way he held it toward Elias, and the way Elias gritted his teeth and tried to move away, I knew it was one that would kill him.

"Please," continued Sterling in his deep, monotone drawl. "Won't you have a seat?"

Elias struggled in Sterling's grasp, his stormy blue eyes gleaming with so much anguish it broke my heart. "Harper, get out! Run!"

Sterling's expression soured and he pushed the orb of light closer to Elias, who shied away, breathing rapidly through clenched teeth.

I didn't dare move.

I wouldn't leave him. An image of the sigil I would need to block an attack came into my mind. But Sterling was an experienced witch, he wouldn't need to draw sigils anymore. He would be able to conjure them simply by thought. I likely wouldn't have enough time to block if he decided to attack me.

My magic started to nip at my flesh, but I held it back. Let it build. This time, I wanted it to get out of control. To cause an earthquake, or a storm, or a damned tornado. It might've been the only way we would get out of this alive.

"I'm not going anywhere," I said, casting an apology at Elias.

"What do you want?" I directed at Sterling.

The Headmaster's dark eyes fell. "It isn't what *I* want," he replied in a deadpan voice. When he raised his eyes to meet mine again, they were churning with something like torment. Narrowed with fury. "It's what must be done."

I shook my head, taking a step closer. "No, please. You don't have to——"

"Does my niece know anything about this? Does anyone else?" he interrupted, his grip on Elias tightening. Elias cringed and I caught sight of the spark of magic at the fingertips of his left hand. He was mounting for an attack of his own.

No! I wanted to shout at him. *Don't try to be a hero, you'll get yourself killed!* My chest and throat tightened.

Distract him. I had to distract him if Elias had any chance of succeeding.

I stepped closer again, and Sterling stiffened, his jaw flexing under his salt and pepper beard. "No," I said. "They know nothing." And suddenly I was so relieved I hadn't told Bianca. Cringing to think of what he might've done to his own niece if I had.

"Good," he replied, and I could see his mind became made up. He fell silent.

"You won't get away with it," I blurted, my gaze darting to Elias.

He gave me the slightest nod. *Keep going,* he

seemed to be saying. A sigil grew from his palm, glowing bright violet.

"You'll—you'll pay for what you did to my father. You'll rot in Kalzir!"

Sterling sighed, hanging his head. "No," he said, and sounded almost disappointed. "I don't think I will."

Elias attacked. With bared teeth and every muscle in his body taught, he fired the spell at Sterling. The Headmaster released him and raised his arm. A hastily conjured shield blocked Elias' blow, but sent him sailing backward. He crashed into the wrought iron table, struggling to right himself.

The sigil he'd had in his hand pulsed with blazing light.

Elias came barreling toward me, and I barely had time to process what was happening before my body was airborne and we landed hard in the tall grass outside the cabin.

The door was blown off its hinges a split second after we'd passed through it. Bits of singed and broken wood rained down around us.

Elias shielded me from the worst of it, shuffling to his feet. He hauled me up with him, and I cried out. My hip twinged when I tried to put weight on my left leg and my elbow stung when the cold night air met raw skin.

"Go!" Elias bellowed, releasing me and turning

back to the cabin, sigils forming around his hands. The feel of his power awakened my own magic back to a violent roar. The savage force of it rushed in my ears. Near deafening.

"Not without you!"

He muttered something under his breath, but I didn't catch what it was. Sterling appeared in the doorway, magic at the ready, dancing along his fingers. Elias didn't hesitate. He catapulted an attack spell at Sterling. It rocketed through the air toward him in a twisting spiral of multicolored light.

Sterling met Elias' attack with one of his own. The two sigils collided in mid-air. Exploded in vivid color, throwing sparks into the night.

Elias attacked again. And Sterling countered. I watched as the force of the headmaster's advances pushed Elias. His feet dug into the ground with the effort of trying not to be blown back.

I drew the sigil for shield and rammed my forearm into it, effectively binding it to me just in time to shield myself from a barrage of magical debris crashing over me like a wave. We wouldn't last long like this. Not without me knowing how to defend myself.

Come on! I urged my powers, trying to visualize lightning raining down from the sky and onto the silver-haired head of Atticus Sterling. But I'd never been able to control when my magic went haywire, or what it did. *Hell*, I didn't even believe I could conjure a storm, no matter what Ms. Granger and Bianca said.

A flash of silver and I saw Fallon slinking around the edge of the cabin, looking for a change to attack Sterling. "No!" I hissed at the fox, and it lifted it's narrow face to hiss back at me. The fox would only get hurt. It would die if it tried to intervene, and Elias could be distracted. "Get out of here," I shouted at it over the *crackle* and *boom* of traded magical attacks. "Go find help!"

I didn't think the fox would listen, or understand what I meant, but it looked from it's bonded witch and back to me and then took off toward the academy. Smart animal.

"Help!" I shouted back through the trees at our backs, toward where the academy peeked through the branches, looking down us.

Someone should've heard us by now. But not a single window shone with light. And no one came.

A bolt of magic snaked out from Elias and Sterling's traded volleys of attack and I saw it. A warding spell surrounded the cabin, stretching at least twenty feet in each direction in a dome-like circle. I was in such a rush I hadn't noticed when I'd passed through. I'd been too panicked. Frantic to get to Elias.

It didn't matter how loud I yelled. If I screamed.

No one would hear me. No one would come to help us.

Elias cried out and I turned in time to see him fall. He was blown back by the strength of Sterling's spell. Stunned. His head connected with the earth and snapped back. His eyes closed.

Sterling lifted his hands to deliver the killing blow, charging up the amber sigil he was about to let fly.

Time slowed.

I bolted toward Elias and it was as though I was running through deep water. Unable to make my legs move any faster. Sterling hurtled the sigil at Elias and I dove.

The spell struck my shield and I had to clutch onto Elias to hold myself and my shield in place, a broken scream tore from my lungs at the burning sensation biting at my raised arm. I fed more power into the shield. I needed it to be stronger.

It had to protect us both. Elias laid still beneath me. His eyes sealed and his face streaked with soot and dirt. Flashes of light illuminated him with each attack launched at us.

Tears blurred the image of him. I felt hopeless. And furious. Completely unhinged.

The sky groaned overhead, and the earth buckled beneath my skinned knees. A tremor rolled over the earth. It was like an opening. As though someone cleaved my chest in two and all the magic inside came pouring out.

Somewhere deep in the woods trees fell, dropping to the earth with resounding booms and crashes. Lightning snaked across the sky above, forking out in all directions—Illuminating the paled face of Headmaster Sterling as he stared in awe of the coming storm, widening his stance to keep his balance on the shaking ground.

A lancing pain shot through my skull, and my shield weakened. But Sterling had already stopped the assault, and now stood staring at me in absolute horror.

Another stab of pain had me curling my hands into tight fists. My fingernails carved little half-moons into my palms. A hot liquid dripped over my lips and when I swallowed I tasted the coppery tang of blood.

Elias' eyes fluttered open, but they remained unfocused. He was coming to. He was alright! I could've shouted with joy. Wanted to burst into tears. But I couldn't do either of those things because Sterling was advancing, moving his hands around a three-dimensional sigil as it built in size and strength.

It looked like a sigil within a sigil within another sigil. I'd never seen anything like it. But I didn't have to know what it was to understand that my shield wouldn't withstand it.

I grabbed Elias' limp hand in mine and whispered, "I'm so sorry."

"You really are your father's daughter," Sterling spat, stopping only a few meters from where I knelt over Elias in the grass. He looked disgusted, but not at me, or at Elias. His face was reddened and twitching. His eyes shone with tears.

He didn't want to do this.

But there was firm intent there, too. He'd already made up his mind. *No loose ends...* The Magistrate had ordered him. And he would comply.

Another wave of magic left me and I recoiled at the release. The earth split around me, fracturing out in every direction except the one I wanted it to go. I couldn't control it. I couldn't save us.

This whole mess happened because I wanted to know what happened to my father. And now I was going to die without even knowing?

Fuck that.

"Why?" I hissed at him. "Why did you kill him?"

Sterling was breathing hard, and the pulsating orb between his weathered hands was nearly ready to be wielded. He wouldn't be able to hold it much longer. Power like that couldn't be contained. I should know.

Lightning struck the ground near the academy, and the atmosphere came alive with light and electricity. The sky opened up and rain fell, thick and heavy, pounding the dirt around us. Soaking through my clothes in seconds and chilling me all the way to the bone.

"He always was too curious for his own good," Sterling shouted over the steading rushing of the rain. "A family trait I think," he added, staring pointedly at me, lowering his brows. "Even his cousin couldn't mind his own damned business. Cost me a history professor in the middle of the year!"

But the history professor who taught here before Elias had died of a heart attack, hadn't he? I was so certain I remembered Elias telling me that. And Bianca telling me how every student in the academy turned out for his funeral. She said he was everyone's favorite. And he was my relative?

A loud gasp ending in a strained sob cut through the sound of the rain, and I whipped my head around to find her standing near the trees, at the edge of Sterling's ward.

Bianca had both of her hands clamped over her mouth as though holding back a scream. Her shoulders shook and tears poured freely from her darkened brown eyes. Her fluffy white housecoat was three inches deep in mud, and the mascara had run all the way to her chin in the rain. Her usually voluminous blond waves were weighted down with water and looked raggedy and thin. "You killed Mr. Simmonds?" she breathed, removing her hands to let them hang, shaking at her sides.

How long had she been listening? Had she seen her uncle attacking Elias and I?

"You killed Harper's dad?" she asked, her voice edging in a shout. Her hot breath clouded around her face in the frigid air. She seemed unbothered by the fact that he held a death-sentence worth of magic in his hands.

Sterling went green. His magic waned, and his chin quivered at the sight of her. He looked like he might be ill.

"Answer me!" Bianca cried. Her voice a high-pitched, blaring scream.

I shook Elias. "Wake up," I whispered. "You need to wake up!" He choked a little, whimpered, but was still unable to move.

Sterling bent his head. His hands trembled around the glowing amber orb. Then they turned to claws and he growled, baring his yellowed teeth as he shouted. "This is all *your* fault!" His crazed voice echoed through the air, and he set his sights on me.

His eyes glinted in the moonlight, exposing the madness dwelling deep within. He raised his hands and I fell to cover Elias' body with my own. Bracing for impact.

But a feral growl pierced the wind, reverberating deep in my core.

I saw him a fraction of second after I heard him. Adrian's wolf came barrelling through the ward and launched himself at Sterling. His strong hind legs propelled him through the air like a loosed arrow. He was a blur of coiled muscle and grayish silver fur.

One second Sterling had a throat. The next, he didn't.

20

His lifeless body slumped to the ground.

Cal loped into view behind Adrian, snarling, his hackles raised high along his spine. Bianca dropped to her knees like a stone and vomited into the grass. Cal growled at her, but I shouted at him. "Cal!" He turned, his ears pricking. "Leave her."

The pounding in my chest began to slow, and with it the rain also slowed. Stopping entirely after only a few seconds.

"Bianca," I called, not wanting to leave Elias' side. In truth, I wasn't sure I could make my legs move even if I wanted them to. My entire left side throbbed, and my legs felt as though they were made of lead. As though they'd sprung root and attached themselves to earth. No, I wouldn't be moving any time soon.

Bianca held up a hand to silence me, and I saw her body racking with sobs. She needed space. She needed to process. And then after, I would tell her what I knew. Explain the ugly truth to her in as much detail as she wanted. Or not at all if she asked.

Elias' eyelids fluttered, and a ragged breath left his lips. He was coming to.

He was going to be alright, I could feel it. His body was already healing. We just had to get him inside and wake Granger. She would know what to do.

Elias's eyes blinked open and his pupils constricted at the onslaught of moonlight. "Hey," I said as calmly as I could, brushing the stray dark hairs away from his face. "It's over. We're safe... we're safe."

He drifted back out of consciousness, sighing as he went as though giving in to the dark only because he now knew I was alright.

Adrian came closer and I shied away at first, seeing his muzzle matted with still-wet blood. He whimpered, and bowed his head, nuzzling against my side. Cal came to join his pack mate. His green eyes roved over me, sniffing the air around my body to check for injury, growling every time he found one.

It took a moment, but once the buzzing of raw power that had been coursing through me ebbed away, seeping back into the earth from where it came, I felt it. Relief flooded every neuron in my body. And when Cal bowed his head to me, I realized what it was.

They'd accepted the bond.

I looked into a set of large glowing golden eyes, and a set of green, and saw something I never thought I'd be able to see in my familiars. Devotion. Hope. And something like desire.

I turned my attention squarely at Adrian and leaned my head against his, feeling his thick fur against my forehead. "Thank you," I whispered.

21

———

*I*t'd been a week since the carnage
outside Elias' cabin.

So much had changed since then. So many
things had happened. Elias was back to his regular
brooding, infuriatingly handsome self after only two
days of missed classes. My familiars had come to
check on me only once since they left the day after
the incident.

They were trying to figure out a way to tell
Atlas, their Alpha, that they'd been bonded to a
witch without having him want to kill me. So far,
they hadn't managed to come up with anything.

I was so glad they'd accepted the bond—
accepted *me*, but they were still under the rule of
their pack leader. They had to follow his command,
whether they liked it or not.

I told them I'd find a way to tell people, too, as soon as everything calmed down at the academy. I couldn't have my familiars being attacked if they were seen on the grounds. It wouldn't stay a secret forever. But, to keep my sanity, I needed it to for at least a few more days.

All that mattered to me right now was that they'd decided to stay. To accept the bond. It brought me so much inner peace. And when I'd seen them on Tuesday, they'd seemed in better spirits, too. Relief was evident in the soft set of their shoulders. Adrian actually *smiled*. He was quick to cover it up, but I saw it, just for a second.

Don't get me wrong. They weren't happy by any stretch of the word. We fought most of the time they were here.

They still loathed witches, and on some level resented the bond and what they perceived it as. That wouldn't change overnight. But they were trying, and that was all I could ask.

I analyzed the formal letter in my hand for the umpteenth time.

I still wasn't sure if I'd made the right choice. Something told me to keep my mouth shut about the Magistrate's involvement in the murder of my father and his cousin, Mr. Percival Simmonds. And in the attempted murder of me and Elias.

It was one thing to accuse a dead man of a

crime. It was quite another to accuse the Magistrate of the Arcane Council of being the one who orchestrated the attacks. So, I told the Arcane Authorities when they came that Atticus Sterling admitted to killing my father and he tried to kill me, and I didn't know why.

Both Bianca and Elias corroborated my story.

I was the only one who knew of the Magistrate's involvement—though I was sure Elias suspected something—and I would keep it that way. For now.

The Arcane Authorities had taken my statement and told me to prepare for trial before the Arcane Council. *And* that the Enduran shifter who'd 'lent his assistance' would have to attend trial, too. They had no idea the real reason Adrian killed Sterling was to save the witch he was bonded to.

Hell, I still had absolutely no idea how to even begin to tell people that...

But it seemed the Magistrate had no intention of allowing this case to go to trial. The letter Bianca and I received the day before explained the trial had been canceled. It stated the council had found enough evidence to support our testimonies and the issue would be laid to rest.

It was signed, Godric Montgomery. The Magistrate himself.

I threw the letter into the trash bin beside Bianca's vanity, my stomach turning in disgust. A soft knock at the door sent a tremor down my spine, and I rushed to open it.

Elias stood solemnly on the other side, that worried crease in his forehead deeper than ever. His raincloud eyes were sympathetic. From behind him stepped Ms. Granger and I swallowed hard. It was time.

I closed the door quietly behind me, not wanting to wake Bianca.

"Are you sure you're ready for this?" Elias asked me, his hands twitching as though he longed to reach out to me but couldn't.

I nodded and righted my navy-blue headband, tucking a loose strand of red hair back in.

"It can still be put off," Ms. Granger added, her voice full of strength and authority.

The woman was ready to take on the world. Since the death of Sterling, the council had appointed her temporary headmaster in his stead. It seemed she was the most qualified for the position, which was the criteria they used in such circumstances.

I didn't think she'd hold the position long, since, you know, the council was full of patriarchal twits with deeply ingrained misogynistic attitudes. But she was determined to keep the position, nonetheless.

If she did, she would be the first ever female

headmistress, and the youngest one, too, if I wasn't mistaken.

"No, I'm ready," I replied to them both, straightening my spine and taking a deep, cleansing breath.

Granger nodded, and when she turned to lead us to the portal in the main office, Elias fell into step beside me. He brushed his fingers over the back of my hand, making gooseflesh rise like a wave up my arm and over the back of my neck.

I glanced back at the dorm room. Bit the inside of my cheek. I didn't like leaving Bianca. She'd hardly left her bed and refused to go back home again.

She'd returned to the mansion in Oregon only to tell her brothers what happened in person and gather some things. Nothing had been officially decided about what was to happen to Sterling's estate and his mass of wealth. So, for the time being, the days passed as they always had in the Sterling household; without him.

Bianca hadn't said as much—hadn't said much of anything at all—but I knew she loathed being there. And, well, pretty much loathed everything right now. She only left her bed to eat and shower, and even those things she didn't do often.

Elias said I should give her space and time to heal. But I hated seeing her that way. She was always happy, smiling, bubbling with life. I didn't recognize this broken shell of girl she'd become and it worried me.

"We should be back within the hour," Elias said reassuringly. He was always reading my mind like that. Seeming to know exactly the words I needed to hear. "The origin spell won't take long to perform."

I didn't care how long it took. I just needed it to tell the council what I already knew to be true; that Alistair Hawkins was my father. It was the only way for me to gain access to his estate property.

I would need access to find out what information was worth killing him over. If he'd kept anything, it could still be in there, in his home. There could be clues... or *something*. There had to be something there, right?

We stepped into Sterling's office, or what was now Granger's office. She'd already cleaned out some things and changed the drapes to a pretty purple. A smile tugged at my lips. She looked *right* in there.

Being headmistress suited her.

She began to open the portal, glancing back to make sure we were both ready to go through. I looked to Elias, who nodded at me. I nodded back. I didn't know he was planning to request permission to attend with us, but I wasn't surprised to see him there outside my door with Granger either. Of course, he'd come.

"Once we step through, we'll be entering directly into the Department of Arcane Inquiry," Granger said, finishing up the sigil. "We're a bit early, so be prepared to wait a while."

The portal opened up on a dimly lit room. Hushed murmurs sounded in the shadows. It was mandatory for two council members to attend the casting of an origin spell, to oversee and document its veracity. But there were definitely more than two people in the room.

I licked my lips and swallowed down the urge to turn and run away. What if I was wrong? What if somehow Alistair Hawkins wasn't my father? I shook my head.

Don't be ridiculous. You know he's your father.

Ms. Granger stepped through first and beckoned for me to follow her. Elias brought up the rear, coming through the portal an instant before it fell closed.

"What is this?" Granger asked, her voice firm as she surveyed all the faces in the circular chamber.

In the middle was a raised platform. A pedestal table sat at its center. And all around the room were council members, sitting behind one enormous, raised desk. Looking down at us with cautious, curious stares.

There were seven of them. S*even* of the eleven remaining council members had come to attend the origin spell. That didn't seem right. Didn't they have better things to do? It was only mandatory that two attend the proceeding.

The council member at the center of the raised desk, a balding man with a mustache, grumbled. "We haven't got time to waste," he said, narrowing his milky gaze at me. "You. Girl, step forward."

I did as asked, moving to stand on the raised platform. A single shaft of sunlight illuminated the pedestal table in a perfect triangle of light. "You have requested a trial of origin, is this correct?"

"Yes," I replied, my voice wavering.

"Do you understand the dangers, implications, and side-effects possible during the administration of an origin spell?"

I hesitated. Side-effects? I knew the information gleaned from an origin spell was irrevocable. And I knew it could be dangerous, and painful. He must've been referring to the exhaustion Elias had already warned me about. "Yes."

"Very well. You may proceed."

Granger was to perform the actual spell. She was the most adept at sigils, and from what I understood, the spell was very complex. She'd been called to do this type of trial for the council before.

Elias moved to stand at the edge of the platform, where he would be in my line of sight. His jaw clenched, and a muscle twitched at his temples. He clasped his hands behind his back, and I saw his biceps bulge under his sharp suit jacket.

Ms. Granger walked up to the balding man and reached up to accept the small vial he handed her. The origin spell required all three main forms of alchemical magic to work. A potion. A sigil. And an incantation.

She brought the vial to me, moving to stand on the opposite side of the small table. The streaks of bronze in her hair glowed umber in the sunlight filtering down on us. And her warm gaze calmed the erratic thrumming in my chest.

"It'll only hurt for a few moments," she said, as though she somehow knew what it felt like. "Then we'll all see your bloodline. It's different for everyone—what the spell shows. But it's always definitive."

I nodded, my nails digging into my palms. "I'm ready."

She handed me the potion, and I considered the reddish colored substance within. It seemed almost alive, the way it shimmered and pirouetted within the vile. I blew out a breath and tipped the contents back, trying not to think about how the taste reminded me of blood and rot.

It took only seconds to start to work. My magic

rushed into me, surging and swaying. The potion pulling it to the surface, keeping it in a lulled, trance-like state beneath my skin. And then the burning started. First in my chest, and then in my legs. My shoulders. My arms. All the way to my toes and fingertips. My veins were *on fire.*

I clenched my teeth, sucking in a breath that sounded more like a whimper. *Just a few minutes.* I only had to withstand it for a few minutes.

Granger began to draw the sigil, taking great care to get each and every line, curve, and shape exactly right. When she was finished, light flared out from its center in brilliant undulating branches of red and gold. She reached for my arm, and I gave it to her, letting it rest against the table.

I was not the type to become faint at the sight of blood, but I found myself turning away as she dragged the runed dagger across my forearm and spoke the ancient incantation. "Originis veritatem."

The spell echoed through the chamber, entering me, swirling through my core until I came unbound. My feet left the floor, and vaguely, I felt the blood dripping down my arm, but I was blinded by pure white light. My head was light and spinning.

The first image came slowly, like a developing photograph in an old Polaroid camera. I saw him first as a man, and then as a boy, and then as a babe.

My father in all his stages of life. I sobbed through the burning and the onslaught of images.

I berated myself for believing for even a second that I was wrong about him being my father.

Then the images came faster, showing his mother before him, and her parentage, and her family, and their family before that. Faster and more violently, the images came.

Back, back, and back my bloodline went. Until there was a woman on a ship, crazed and in chains. And then a man before her, laughing as he burned. The final image was of a man, dripping wet as he hauled himself out of a turbulent white-capped sea onto craggy black stones. His eyes were bright green and frenzied, and his hair was red as flame. On his breast, he bore an insignia of two swords in a rose.

The burning peaked, and I screamed, falling back to the ground in a heap as the magic of the spell left me all at once. Detaching from my body in one great ripping pull.

There was an outbreak of astonished whispering, and I fought to regain my vision, recoiling when someone tried to help me stand.

"It's only me," Elias said, and I let him drag my arm around his neck and lift me so my weight rested against his side.

"It's impossible," I heard one of the council members say.

"That bloodline ended with Cyprian over a thousand years ago!" another shouted.

I heard Granger asking for them to calm down. Calling for order.

As my vision began to clear, I found Elias's eyes staring down at me. My head lolled to the side. I was barely able to hold it up.

"What is it?" I asked him, my voice weak. "What happened?"

His lips parted and his breaths shallowed. "It can't be," he replied, looking at me as though I was something other than the girl he knew. Like I was a foreign creature he'd never seen before.

Like I was... dangerous.

Follow Harper's story in OF MAGIC & MOONLIGHT, Arcane Arts Academy Book 2!
Get it here: mybook.to/OMAM